Claudine's House

Claudine's House

Colette

Translated by Andrew Brown

ET REMOTISSIMA PROPE

Modern Voices

Modern Voices
Published by Hesperus Press Limited
4 Rickett Street, London SW6 1RU
www.hesperuspress.com

Claudine's House first published in French as *La Maison de Claudine* in 1922
This translation first published by Hesperus Press Limited, 2006

This book is supported by the French Ministry for Foreign Affairs, as part of
the Burgess programme headed for the French Embassy in London by the
Institut Français du Royaume-Uni

Designed by Fraser Muggeridge studio
Typeset by William Chamberlain
Printed in Jordan by Jordan National Press

ISBN: 1-84391-415-8

Contents

Foreword

Claudine's House was written when Colette was no longer subject to M. Willy, her husband and jailer (they had been separated since 1906). He had always been urging her to 'spice things up a little' – to him her writings had only one use, to earn money. She had resisted, and we may be sure he would not have welcomed a sad memoir. Throughout her life she did sound notes of loss and sadness, talking about her mother, her mother's life, but there is nothing of that here.

We know all about unhappy childhoods; you could say we specialise in them, to the point where some, upon hearing 'I had such a happy childhood', have been known to protest: 'Then you must have forgotten.'

Colette's memoirs of her childhood are for some of us a reminder of what could have been. She was a child in paradise, presided over by a goddess of love and harmony, her mother Sido. There are no photographs of Sido, and that is as it should be. And I could have done without Colette's description of her: a dumpy red-cheeked little woman with rough hands… No, I prefer my imagination unfettered by fact. But I may dream of a tall calm Demeter-like figure as much as I like: Colette's childhood paradise was made possible by an often impatient, busy country woman who had the gift of absorbing difficulty and discord and creating kindness.

Colette longed for her mother always, and particularly when first married and immured in Paris. The idyll ended when Colette was twelve, but she does not dwell on what must have been a tragedy for the family – no room for tears in these smiling memoirs. She does no more than hint at the money troubles and discords that had to end the life in that house. She must have been so painfully aware of the differences between her difficult second life and the one described so nostalgically in this book, where happiness is boundless, spreading along streets and gardens, all under the same beneficent spell.

When Sido visits Paris, she returns to the house – which is a hundred miles from Paris, but could be in another realm altogether – to say she could not bear to live where there were no dogs to greet you, going out and coming in, no cats, none of the vigorous animal life of a village; where a cat or a dog or a horse is known to everyone like a neighbour; where birds, insects, the weather provide the dramas of the everyday.

In Sido's Eden the extraordinary was commonplace. A cat's favourite sleeping place was on top of the birdcage; the birds being so little discommoded by this enemy – which they apparently did not know was one – that they would tweak a hair to line a nest. A rabbit with the heart of a lion vigorously defended his mistress when he thought she was under threat, and Colette's dog carried scars to prove it. Above Sido's bed, a large spider (in shape like a clove of garlic, marked with a cross) pursued its life in a web that was permitted to stay in a high corner of the bedroom. Sido liked a cup of chocolate by her bed, kept warm by a glimmering night light. She would lie and watch the great spider let itself down over the cup and drink its fill of the sweet draught, and then it ascended, slowly, because of its load of nectar.

Colette was Sido's favourite child, her 'Minet-Chéri', ('Little-Darling'), her sunshine, her triumph, her achievement, but, as has to be in a fairy tale, there was a bad presence, the elder half-sister, dark and saturnine, and with 'Mongol' eyes. She read novels day and night, lived entirely on dreams, and was a stranger in this blessed house. She married unwisely and cut off relations with her family. And why did she do this? She did not forgive carelessness with money, which meant there would be no inheritance for her. Her hair, like Colette's, was never cut, and here is a hint of the disquieting, the dubious: why would Sido refuse to cut her two daughters' hair, though brushing and braiding the young heads wore her out? 'I've had enough… my left leg hurts… I've just been combing Juliette's hair,' she would plead, collapsing. When Colette, at Willy's command, did have her hair cut, Sido complained that he had destroyed her labour of love. When the unhappily married daughter is incarcerated by her wicked husband we expect her to let her braids down over the garden wall so that a rescuer may climb up them.

Claudine's House's dreamy sentences may beckon and promise, but, when alerted by some half-hint or suggestion, one has to realise that the good and benevolent lives side by side with misfortune. This other, darker, parallel life would become visible when Colette once consulted a fortune-teller who told her that her dead father was present, unseen by Colette, sitting there in a corner, unable to take his eyes off his successful daughter, whom he has always envied as a result of her becoming what he had always wanted to be, a writer. When her father died, his family found beautiful books, with enticing titles and sheets of stiff, gleaming creamy-white paper – but they were blank; he had been unable to write. Sido used the glossy pages to make covers for her jams and preserves. This detail is painful, as though she was trying to conceal her husband's failure. Why not secretly burn them? But what thrifty woman could have brought herself to do that?

The father, Captain Colette, had only one leg, having lost the other one on the battlefield, and he was handsome and brave. He also flirted with women, but he adored his wife so much the children often felt they were in the way of this great passion. But he did lose his wife's inheritance, he did impoverish her, and Colette regrets that she did not ask him a thousand questions when he was alive, because he died with many secrets.

It was not only her dead father who haunted Colette – perhaps not as a ghost, which the rationalist Colette would have dismissed, but certainly as a reminder of unanswered questions – her younger brother visited her too. He was the child who adored music so much that he would follow a travelling band for miles and, grown-up, would not take a real job because that would get in the way of his music. 'An elf of sixty-three,' as once Colette said; he would drop in to his famous sister's flat to say, 'I've been *there* again, you know.' 'You haven't! Tell me, tell me!' And the two elderly people would sit and remember the ancient gate, that always creaked, and long-dead animals and people, and, of course, that voice – 'that beautiful young voice' – which told them, 'Look, just look – do you see?' That bright wasp on a sticky translucent plum, the blackbird holding a cherry in his claw just so, the cat with her nose tucked into her paws because she knows it is going to be cold.

What a pleasure this book is, making you dream of that old house in its garden, just as Colette did, all her life.

– *Doris Lessing, 2006*

Introduction

Despite its title, this is not one of the series of 'Claudine' novels (*Claudine at School*, *Claudine in Paris*, *Claudine Married* and *Claudine Takes Off*, published successively from 1900 to 1903) that made Colette famous – or rather (to begin with at least) made her first husband Willy (Henri Gauthier-Villars) famous, since he published them under his own name. The story of how Willy, the journalist, popular novelist and *belle époque* bon vivant exploited a team of workers (including his young wife) to produce work that he then passed off as his own is well known, as is the phenomenal success of the Claudine novels that to some extent were a fictionalised version of aspects of Colette's life, much adorned with imaginary titillating and salacious detail. 'Claudine' became Colette's alter ego: the model for an emancipated lifestyle, a fullness of sensual and emotional experience and a courageous defiance of convention. But *Claudine's House* was written much later, in 1922. Although Colette intriguingly gives it the name of her fictional double in the title (curiously, she was simultaneously writing a novel called *The Double*, eventually published as *The Second Woman*), she nowhere uses the name 'Claudine' in the actual text, where she is 'Colette' (or more usually '*Minet-Chéri*', 'Little-Darling', or '*La Petite*', 'Little One'). By the time she wrote this work, Colette had long since come into her own, even if (as the retention of the name 'Claudine' in the title suggests) this is no straightforward autobiography. It mingles fact and fiction and tempers the innocence of Little-Darling with the knowledge and experience of the mature Colette. With the lightest of touches, Colette indicates what the future holds in store for Little-Darling. For instance, the latter proclaims that she wants to be a sailor, and 'does sometimes dream of being a boy and wearing a blue beret and trousers' – a laconic signalling of Colette's androgyny (she would play *travesti* roles on stage, and be a lover of women as well as men). Indeed, *Claudine's House* is a series of superbly economical sketches in which many of the themes that Colette explores at greater length in her fictional works are adumbrated: love, the pleasures of the senses, the close and yet enigmatic world of animals. Here she is liberated from the constraints of narrative, free to explore the anecdotal, to evoke atmosphere, to describe the repetitive rituals of rural life and summon up a childhood that is timeless in the sense of being atemporal: urgent but unfocused, ardent and yet free-floating. Social roles are as yet relatively undefined, and yet boundaries count: village life, even for children, is full of taboos, lines that cannot be crossed with impunity, suffused by a sense of property and propriety that the young Colette acknowledges even though the mature Colette has succeeded in breaking through them. Human and animal can merge (Colette's cats and dogs can 'speak') and yet any anthropomorphism is limited by an acknowledgement of animals' otherness. She manages to combine a realistic awareness of the objectivity of everyday life, the way it resists the self's devices and desires, with an equal recognition that – especially in childhood, and maybe in a rural childhood more than in an urban setting – the world is imbued with the fantastic. There are ghosts in the attic, maybe, and tombstones in the garden. Visitors from outside the village are endowed with an almost supernatural aura. The peasant who sings at Adrienne's wedding ('The Wedding') comes from another small town: 'Just think! A man who lives in Dampierre-sous-Bouhy! At least thirty kilometres from here!' Thirty kilometres: another world. The survivors of far-flung wars drift into the village on the tides of history: one of them is Colette's own father, Captain Jules Colette, an ex-Zouave who had fought in Algeria and Turkey and the Crimea (Alma, Sebastopol) and lost his leg at the Battle of Marignano in Italy. The distant sound of the trumpets and drums of war is faintly audible in this rural retreat, as if in some *Lied* by Mahler. And when Sidonie ('Sido', Colette's mother) is brought by her first husband, the 'Savage', from the sophistication and urbanity of Brussels (where she had been raised) to the isolated village of Saint-Sauveur in Burgundy, she too encounters what is in effect another world, where 'wicked fairies with hairy chins darted a glance at the new wife, which cast an evil spell on her'. Still, for all its similarity to other evocations of provincial life (such as Alain-Fournier's *Le Grand Meaulnes*), *Claudine's House* is not set in some dreamlike *France profonde*, but among a gossipy, alert, observant populace. Both the Captain and Sido (who married him after the death of the 'Savage') were relatively freethinking characters, and though they soon put down roots in Saint-Sauveur, Sido in particular was, for her time, a remarkably emancipated woman; her early life in Brussels was cosmopolitan, even bohemian, and she was almost certainly influenced by Victor Considérant, the disciple of the French utopian writer Fourier. She thought of herself as a woman born three hundred years too early: at all events, she may have communicated to her daughter some of Fourier's attentiveness to the life of the senses.

This sensuality in Colette's writing (her 'style') is highly seductive, and gains an added edge from a sense both of pleasure's evanescence and of the way the sheer amorphous intensity particular to childhood experience poses a problem for the mature writer. As so often in autobiographical writing, Colette registers a sense of melancholy at the inadequacy of language to capture the past. 'Is it worth my describing the rest?' she asks ('Where are the Children?'). 'Words are so inadequate.' And: 'House and garden are still alive, I know; but of what avail is that, if their magic has deserted them, and their secret has been lost – the secret that once opened up a whole world to me: light, different scents, the harmony of trees and birds, the murmur of human voices that death has already stilled… a world of which I am no longer worthy?' This sense of a fall from relatively pre-verbal innocence into articulate and at times disabused experience is qualified by the acknowledgement that childhood was never merely innocent, that Little-Darling was in many ways a very self-aware young girl, and that language, which seems to break the sensuous organic unity of the child's world into lifeless atoms, can also attempt to repair that damage. The shattered wholeness can be restored, its shards reassembled in new combinations that, even if only indirectly, enable the mind to re-enact the perplexing, terrifying and exhilarating intensities of childhood. Some of Colette's images are startling in their power to recapture the past by estranging us from the routines of the present, and they paradoxically rediscover the visionary powers of the child even in the act of lamenting their loss: 'the terrifying moonlight will never return in its silver, leaden-grey and mercury hues, with its razor-sharp facets of amethyst, its cutting, wounding sapphires, seen through a certain pane of blue glass in the summer-house at the bottom of the garden' ('Where are the Children?'). Hugh Shelley suggests that this is actually a reference to the sunlight seen through the blue glass, as if the shattering power of the sun can be seen only indirectly, in the lunar glow of memory. There is a discreet surrealist in Colette, just as there is a prose poet, akin to Francis Ponge (especially in her vibrant but disconcertingly defamiliarised images of animals and plants). Words and things have not yet become monoga-mously wedded to one another: they can still play the field before settling down (if they ever do). Little-Darling is strangely attracted to the word 'presbytery', overheard in an adult conver-sation: instead of asking her parents what it means, the girl dwells on its texture (it's like a piece of coarse embroidery) and its sound (in French, *presbytère* has 'a long-drawn-out, dreamy final syllable'): she carries the word onto the garden wall as if it were a thing, and proceeds to apply it to whatever she wants. She is Humpty-Dumpty, who said 'when I use a word, it means just what I choose it to mean – neither more nor less'. So by 'presbytery' she chooses to mean an outlaw being sent into exile, or a certain yellow-and-black striped snail. When forced to realise that 'presbytery' means the place where a priest lives, she 'compromises' with reality. The referent is lost (she tries to hug the rags and tatters of her 'eccentric ideas' to herself a little longer, but is forced to chuck away the broken fragments of the snail shell), but unlike Humpty-Dumpty she can pick herself up after her great fall and re-ascend her wall – which she promptly rebaptises as *her* presbytery. For she is, as the title of this episode tells us, 'the priest on the wall' – the priest of language. This anecdote, a page or so long, is far more complex, delicate and economical than my cumbrous summary: it is exemplary in its humour, its sense of the dialectic of loss and gain involved in learning what words 'really' refer to and its defiant pride in regaining, at a higher level, the child's ability to make them mean *something else*.

Similar discreet but telling images can be found everywhere. Here is Sido telling Little-Darling about her (Sido's) own father, who had been a chocolate manufacturer in Lyons. 'In those days,' says Sido, 'chocolate was made with cocoa, sugar and vanilla. At the top of the house, bricks of chocolate were laid out on the terrace while still soft, to dry. And every morning, there were slabs of chocolate marked by the imprints – flower shapes with five petals –' The odd synaesthesia of the image here is typical of Colette – a composite of sense-impressions (taste, touch, sight – even though the text doesn't name them directly, it's difficult not to pick up a whiff of felinity superimposed on the warm aroma of chocolate, or a faintly floral scent in the five-petalled cat-paw imprints), which is intensely concrete in its impact. Yet it is allowed (with the politeness that sense-impressions sometimes show towards the concept) to signal an abstraction – for what else are the cats doing but *writing*, leaving their own neat, unmistakeable (and in this case transgressive) trace on a yielding surface? Here too, Colette's mind immediately goes off at a tangent – or rather shuts down. For her memories suddenly cease at just this point, as if she had gone deaf. Her mother Sido is trying to summon up the memory of her own family, but Colette, yet again, is after something else: 'I left my mother to summon up from oblivion the dead people she had loved, while I continued to hang dreamily on a perfume or an image that she had evoked: the odour of the chocolate in its soft bricks, and the hollow flowers that had bloomed under the paws of the wandering cat'. The artist's apparent indifference to her mother's emotion picks up on a concrete image that, in its sensuousness imprinted with meaning, indirectly – and all the more movingly – preserves the lost world of Sido's childhood.

Hence the sense of continuity, survival, the persistence of the past, that qualifies the nagging sense of transience. Sometimes this can take somewhat intriguing forms. Colette's original name (Sidonie-Gabrielle Colette) contained her mother's given name 'Sidonie', and when Colette started to write she used her father's family name as her given name: she then passed on this name, Colette, to her own daughter – as well as the nickname 'Bel-Gazou', which had been one of the nicknames her father, Captain Colette, had given *her*. The nostalgia and melancholy of the later sketches of *Claudine's House*, in which the mature Colette remembers her dead mother and looks rather wistfully at her own daughter ('Colette II' as she sometimes called her) growing up and losing her childhood, is qualified by an uncanny, slightly claustrophobic (or incestuous) sense of continuity across three generations.

But the loss is there all the same, not to be gainsaid. 'Where are the Children?' is almost intolerably poignant. Sido comes out of the house to call her children in. The garden is as strewn with clues as the scene of some crime: an open book here, an abandoned skipping rope or a miniature garden there. But the criminals – the children ('our solitary crime was our silence, and the almost miraculous way we would vanish') – are nowhere to be seen: playing games, hiding in the trees and undergrowth, reluctant to come in for supper. (How terrifying it is, the casual way in which children will hide from an anxious parent and play dead – terrifying, and yet so perfectly natural.) Colette answers her mother's question in several ways. One is: 'nowhere' – the children are gone, for even if at least two of them are still alive, they are gone from their mother – *she* has died, and the question 'Where are the children?' seems to call forth its unstated counterpart, 'Where is our mother?' (While planning this book, she told Martin du Gard, in an interview, that she wanted to rediscover 'her mother', 'the good one': there is a certain restorative idealism at work here, mending the holes in a relationship that was at times as fraught as any living relationship between parent and child must be.) But, as Colette suggests, a less short-sighted mother would have spotted a face in the tree or at the window: the children were there all the time, they had simply blended into their environment, and their mother just needed to look in the right place. So the second answer is 'right in front of your eyes!' A third answer is one that Colette does not state, but enacts in her writing: the children are here, now, in memory, in words, as present as they ever were. But it is a tribute precisely to her tact as a writer that she refuses to give us this equivocal, tentative, problematic answer in unequivocal and abstract language, preferring, as ever, to name the children (even in their absence) in the most embodied of terms: as a whiff of wild garlic, a pocket made wet by bathing trunks, a cut knee and a grazed elbow. In the same way, how vividly is Sido's whole being summed up as the three calluses on her hand, left by the three different gardening tools of this passionate gardener! For from these *disjecta membra*, as from Colette's apparently so unassuming and fragmentary prose sketches, there arise both an integral image of the Good Mother, and the essence of a certain childhood.

– *Andrew Brown, 2006*

Note on the Text:
I have used the edition of *La Maison de Claudine* by Hugh Shelley (London: Harrap & Co., 1964), with its excellent notes, to which the present edition is deeply indebted. It has been a pleasure to consult the beautiful translation by Una Vincenzo Troubridge and Enid McLeod (first published as *My Mother's House* by Martin Secker and Warburg in 1953). My biographical information about Colette is mainly derived from the fine biography by Judith Thurman, *Secrets of the Flesh. A Life of Colette* (London: Bloomsbury, 1999).

Claudine's House

Where are the Children?

It was a big house, surmounted by a high loft. The street rose steeply, which meant that the stables and sheds, the hen-houses, the laundry room and the dairy were obliged to huddle round a closed courtyard at the bottom of the slope.

If I leant up over the garden wall, I could just scratch with my fingertip the roof of the hen-house. The Upper Garden overlooked the Lower Garden, a warm, narrow kitchen garden where aubergines and pimientos were grown, where in July the smell of the tomato leaves mingled with the fragrance of the apricots ripening on the espaliers. In the Upper Garden there were two twin fir trees, a walnut tree whose intolerant shade killed off all the flowers beneath it, roses, neglected stretches of lawn, a tumbledown arbour... At the bottom, a strong iron railing that ran along the rue des Vignes should have ensured that the two gardens were protected from incursions; but I never knew this railing to be anything other than twisted and torn out of the cement of the wall, swept aloft and brandished in mid-air by the invisible arms of a hundred-year-old wisteria...

The main façade was on the rue de l'Hospice: it had a double flight of steps and large, graceless windows pierced its blackened surface. It was the typical bourgeois house of an old village, but its gravity was somewhat undermined by the steep slope of the street, and its flight of steps was lopsided, with four steps on one side and six on the other.

It was a big, serious-looking house, somewhat forbidding with its front-doorbell like that of an orphanage and its carriage entrance with a huge bolt like an ancient dungeon. Only on one side did it smile. Its rear, invisible to the passer-by, lit by the golden sunlight, was swathed in a tangle of wisteria and bignonia branches that weighed down the weary iron trellis that sagged in the middle like a hammock and provided shade for a little flagged terrace and the doorway into the living room… Is it worth my describing the rest? Words are so inadequate. I will never be able to communicate to anyone else the splendour that, in my memory, imbues the red trailers of an autumn vine collapsing under its own weight and clinging, in its fall, to a few fir-tree branches. Those massive lilacs whose compact flowers, blue in the shade and purple in the sunlight, soon withered, suffocated by their own exuberance – those lilacs that died long ago will never, despite all my efforts, rise up again towards the light; the terrifying moonlight will never return in its silver, leaden-grey and mercury hues, with its razor-sharp facets of amethyst, its cutting, wounding sapphires, seen through a certain pane of blue glass in the summer-house at the bottom of the garden.

House and garden are still alive, I know; but of what avail is that if their magic has deserted them and their secret has been lost – the secret that once opened up a whole world to me: light, different scents, the harmony of trees and birds, the murmur of human voices that death has already stilled… a world of which I am no longer worthy?

It sometimes happened that a book, left open on the flags of the terrace or on the grass, a skipping rope snaking down a path, or a tiny garden surrounded by pebbles and planted with the lopped-off heads of flowers, could once upon a time – when this house and this garden harboured a family – reveal the presence of children, and their different ages. But these signs were hardly ever accompanied by the shouting and laughter of children, and the building, warm and full as it was, bore a strange resemblance to those houses that, at the end of the holidays, are suddenly and abruptly divested of all joy. The silence, the low breeze blowing through the walled garden, the pages of the book which the invisible thumb of some sylph kept flicking through, all seemed to be asking: 'Where are the children?'

It was then that, from under the ancient iron trellis sagging to the left under the weight of the wisteria, my mother would appear, still small and plump in those days when age had not yet left her looking thin and bony. She would scrutinise the massive clump of greenery, and then look up and call into the breeze, 'Children! Where are the children?'

Where? Nowhere. Her cry rang across the garden, reverberated off the great wall of the barn, and returned, as a faint and almost imperceptible echo: 'Wheeere… children…'

Nowhere. My mother would throw back her head and gaze up at the clouds, as if she expected a flock of winged children to come swooping down. After a while, she uttered the same cry, then grew weary of questioning the heavens, and with her fingernail broke open a dry poppy-head, scratched a rose-stem dotted with green aphids, dropped the first walnuts into her pocket, shook her head as she brooded over the vanished children, and went back into the house. Meanwhile, in the branches of the walnut tree above, there gleamed down the triangular face of a child lying stretched out like a tomcat along a thick branch, in silence. A less short-sighted mother might have realised that when the twin peaks of the two fir trees exchanged hasty bows, they were being shaken by more than merely the sudden gusts of October wind… And in the square dormer window, above the pulley for hauling up fodder, might she not have spotted, if she screwed up her eyes, those two pale patches standing out against the hay: the face of a young boy, and his book? But she had abandoned her attempt to find out where we were, she had given up any chance of reaching us. No shout or cry accompanied our strange turbulence. I do not think anyone has ever seen children that were livelier and yet more silent. Only now does this surprise me. Nobody had asked us to be so cheerfully mute, or so relatively unsociable. My brother, the one who was nineteen and built hydrotherapy apparatuses from

5

sausage-shaped pieces of cloth, pieces of wire and glass tubes, never stopped his younger brother, who was fourteen, from dismantling a watch, or making a faultless piano reduction of a melody or some symphonic piece he had heard in the nearby town – nor from taking an obscure pleasure in dotting the garden with little tombstones he had cut out of cardboard, each of which bore, under its cross, the names, the epitaph and the genealogy of some imaginary dead person... My sister, who wore her hair too long, could read for as long as she liked, without pausing for rest: the two boys would pass by her as if they did not see her, brushing past the young girl who just sat there, her mind enraptured and far away, without ever disturbing her. When I was little I could, if I wished, follow the boys, almost running after them as they strode along, plunging into the woods in pursuit of red admirals, swallowtails and purple emperors, or hunting for grass snakes, or gathering up armfuls of the tall July foxgloves that grew in the clearings deep in the woods, glowing red with pools of heather... But I tagged along in silence, and picked blackberries, wild cherries, or flowers; I explored the coppices and the waterlogged meadows like a dog who is free and doesn't owe anyone any explanation...

'Where are the children?' She would hail into view like an over-protective mother-bitch breathlessly questing after her young, her head lifted as she sniffed the wind. Her arms with their white cloth sleeves revealed that she had just been kneading the dough for cakes, or a pudding with its velvety hot sauce of rum and jam. She would be wearing a big blue apron round her waist if she had just been washing the Havanese bitch, and sometimes she would be waving a flag of rustling yellow paper, used to wrap up the butcher's meat; she hoped she could gather, at the same time as those children of hers scattered far and wide, her nomadic she-cats, hungry for raw meat...

To her traditional cry she would sometimes add, in the same tone of urgency and supplication, a reminder of what time it was. 'Four o'clock! They haven't come in for tea! Where are the children?...' – 'Half-past six! Are they going to be home for dinner? Where are the children?...' A lovely voice she had: how I would weep for pleasure to hear it again... Our only failing, our solitary crime was our silence, and the almost miraculous way we would vanish. With perfectly innocent plans in mind, intent on a freedom that nobody ever denied us, we would jump over the railing, kicking off our shoes; when we returned, we would climb over a fortuitous ladder, or a neighbour's low wall. Our anxious mother's acute sense of smell would sniff us, picking up a whiff of wild garlic from a distant ravine, or the mint of the marshes that lay concealed under a mantle of grass. One of the boys would have a damp pocket where he had hidden the bathing trunks he'd taken to wear in the fever-filled ponds, and his 'kid sister', with a cut on her knee and a graze on her elbow, would be quite unbothered by the fact that she was still bleeding under plasters of spiders' webs and ground pepper, bound with lengths of entwined grass...

'Tomorrow, I'm going to keep you all locked up! All of you, d'you hear? All of you!'

Tomorrow... Tomorrow, the eldest boy, slipping off the slate roof where he was setting up a water tank, would break his collarbone and lie there, in polite silence, half-fainting, at the foot of the wall, waiting for someone to come and lift him up. Tomorrow the youngest would be whacked right in the middle of his forehead by a six-metre-long ladder; without a word of complaint, he would return home modestly bearing a purple bump as big as an egg between his eyes...

'Where are the children?'

Two are at rest.[1] The others, day by day, are growing older. If there is a place where, after life, we linger waiting, then she who

7

waited for us once is still tremulous with anxiety for the two who are still alive. For the eldest of her daughters, she has at least stopped staring at the dark window pane when evening falls, saying, 'Ah! I feel she's not a happy girl... Ah! I can feel she's suffering...'

For the eldest of the boys she no longer waits, quivering with apprehension as she listens out for the wheels of a doctor's trap coming over the snow at night, nor the tread of the grey mare. But I know that for the two who are left, she continues to wander and seek, invisible, tormented by the idea that she has not kept a close enough watch over them. 'Where can they be? Where are the children?...'

The Savage

When he eloped with her, she was eighteen years old.[2] This was in about 1853; she left behind a family consisting merely of two brothers, French journalists who were married and living in Belgium, and her friends – painters, musicians and poets, a whole crowd of Bohemian youth, of French and Belgian artists. She was a blonde girl, not very pretty but charming with her wide mouth and her delicate little chin, her merry grey eyes, and her hair gathered into a bun that hung low on her neck, where wisps of rebellious hair slipped out from the pins; an independent girl, used to living freely and openly with boys, whether they were brothers or friends. A girl without a dowry, a trousseau or any jewellery, but with a slender figure that curved gracefully above her full skirt: a girl with a neat slender figure and round shoulders, short and stocky.

The Savage saw her, one day when she had travelled from Belgium to France to spend a few weeks over the summer with her nanny from the country. He was on horseback, visiting his neighbouring estates. He was used to loving and leaving his servant-girls, and this offhand young girl who had stared at him without lowering her eyes, and without smiling at him, stayed in his mind. The girl was quite attracted by the passing stranger's black beard, his cherry-red roan, and his distinguished vampire-like paleness, but she had forgotten him by the time he made enquiries about her. He found out her name: she was called 'Sido', short for Sidonie. Like many 'savages' he was a stickler for the formalities, and called on the services of a notary and various relatives, with the result that her family in Belgium learnt that this son of gentlemen glass-blowers owned farms, woods, a fine house with a flight of steps and a garden, and ready cash... Sido listened, panic-stricken and silent, twisting her blond ringlets round her fingers. But a young girl

9

without a fortune or a trade, who is dependent on her brothers for everything, has only one choice: shut up, be grateful for her good luck, and thank God.

So she left the cosy Belgian house, the cellar-kitchen that smelled of gas, warm bread and coffee; she left her piano, her violin, the big Salvator Rosa[3] she had inherited from her father, the tobacco jar and the fine long-stemmed clay pipes, the coke braziers, the books that lay open and the crumpled newspapers, and as a new bride entered the house with its flight of steps, isolated by the harsh winter of the forest lands all around.[4]

Here she found, to her surprise, a white and gold living room on the ground floor, but a first floor with barely even rough-cast walls, as abandoned as a loft. In the stables, two sturdy horses and two cows gorged themselves with forage and oats; butter was churned and cheese pressed in the outbuildings, but the bedrooms were icy-cold and prompted no thoughts of either love or sweet sleep.

There was an abundance of silverware – engraved with the emblem of a goat on its rear hooves – glassware and wine. Shadowy old women sat spinning by candlelight in the kitchen in the evening, stripping and winding off the flax from the estate to provide the beds and the butlery with heavy, hard-wearing, cold linen. The harsh cackle of bickering kitchen-maids would rise and fall depending on whether the master was leaving the house or returning to it; wicked fairies with hairy chins darted a glance at the new wife, casting an evil spell on her, and a pretty laundry maid, tossed aside by her master, sobbed bitterly as she leant against the well, whenever the Savage was away hunting.

This Savage, usually quite a well-mannered fellow, initially treated his civilised little wife well. But Sido, who longed for friends and an innocent and cheerful social life, found on her estate only servants, cunning farmers and gamekeepers caked with wine and the blood of hares, leaving an odour of wolf in their wake. The Savage spoke to them rarely and haughtily. From his faded nobility he retained only disdain, politeness, brutality and the relish of having inferiors; his nickname merely referred to his habit of going out alone on horseback, hunting without a dog or a companion, and saying next to nothing. Sido loved conversation, mockery, movement, a kindness that was authoritarian yet devoted, and gentleness. She filled the big house with flowers, had the dark kitchen whitewashed, oversaw in person the preparation of the Flemish dishes, kneaded cakes with raisins and looked forward to having her first child. The Savage would smile at her between two outings and then set off once more. He returned to his vineyards and his spongy woods, lingering in the taverns at crossroads where just a single long candle pierces the all-encompassing darkness: the rafters, the smoky walls, the rye bread and the wine in the iron tankards...

When she had exhausted her tasty recipes, her patience, and her furniture polish, Sido – who had grown thin with loneliness – started to cry, and the Savage spotted the trace of tears on her face, which she denied shedding. He vaguely realised that she was bored, that she was missing a certain type of comfort and luxury that was quite foreign to all his savage austerity. But what could it be?...

He left on horseback one morning and trotted to the nearest town – forty kilometres away. He tramped all around the streets, and returned the following night, with an awkward air of grandeur and two amazing objects in his hand, bound to fill any yearning young wife with the greatest delight: a little mortar for pounding almonds and dough, made of the rarest lumachella marble,[5] and a cashmere shawl from India.

In the tarnished, cracked mortar I could, if I wished, still pound almonds mixed with sugar and lemon peel. But I have to confess, to my shame, that I cut up the cherry-coloured cashmere shawl to make cushions and handbags. For my mother –

the loveless and innocent Sido of her hypochondriac first husband – took shawl and mortar into her own sentimental keeping and looked after them with the greatest care.

'You see,' she used to tell me, '*he* brought them to me, that Savage who was quite unable to give presents. And yet he took the trouble to bring them to me, tying them to his mare Mustapha. He stood before me, his arms laden, as proud and clumsy as a big dog carrying a tiny slipper in its jaws. And I realised that, in his eyes, his presents were not merely a mortar and a shawl. They were "presents", rare and expensive objects that he had travelled far to find; it was his first unselfish gesture – and, I'm afraid, his last – to cheer up and console a young wife who was in exile, weeping…'

Love

'There's nothing for this evening's dinner… Tricotet still hadn't killed anything this morning… He was going to kill something at midday. I'll go to the butcher's myself. I won't bother to change. What a bore! Oh, why do we have to eat? What are we going to eat this evening?'

My mother is standing by the window, looking very demoralised. She's wearing her sateen 'indoor dress' with polka dots, her silver brooch depicting two angels leaning over the portrait of a child, her glasses are dangling from a chain and her lorgnette is tied to the end of a black silk cord that is forever getting caught on door keys and snagged on drawer knobs so that it needs to be constantly reknotted. She gazes at us, one after the other, hopelessly. She knows that none of us will give her any useful advice. When consulted, Papa will reply:

'Raw tomatoes with plenty of pepper.'

'Red cabbage with vinegar,' Achille would have said – the eldest of my brothers, whose doctorate keeps him busy in Paris.

'A big bowl of chocolate!' Such will be the request of Leo, the second.

And jumping into the air, since I often forget that I'm already over fifteen, I will demand: 'Chips! I want chips! And walnuts with cheese!'

But it seems that chips, chocolate, tomatoes and red cabbage don't 'add up to a dinner'…

'Why not, Maman?'

'Don't ask silly questions…'

She is completely preoccupied. She has already picked up the black rattan basket with lid, and heads off, not bothering to change. She keeps on her wide-brimmed garden hat, scorched by three summers, its narrow crown banded with a maroon ruche, and her gardening apron: the curved beak of her secateurs has made a hole in one of its pockets. In the hollow of her other pocket, some dry nigella seeds in their paper sachet make, as she walks, a sound of raindrops and fingernails scraping silk. Feeling vain on her behalf, I cry, 'Maman, take your apron off!'

She continues to walk, but turns to look at me: her face framed by her parted hair looks weighed down by the sorrows of her fifty-five years – but only thirty when she is feeling cheerful.

'Why? I'm only going to the rue de la Roche.'

'Leave your mother alone,' scolds my father through his beard. 'Anyway, where's she going?'

'To Léonore's, to get dinner.'

'Aren't you going with her?'

'No. I don't feel like it today.'

There are days on which Léonore's butcher's shop – with its knives, its hatchet, its swelling oxen's lungs swaying and irides-cent in the breeze, and pink like the pulpy flower of a begonia – delights me as much as a sweetshop. Léonore always cuts off a ribbon of salted bacon for me and holds it out, dangling from her cold fingertips, transparent. In the garden of the butcher's house, Marie Tricotet – although she was born on exactly the same day as me – still amuses herself by sticking a pin into unemptied pigs' or calves' bladders, and then squashing them under her feet, 'to make the water squirt out'. The horrid sound of skin being stripped from the fresh meat, the roundness of the kidneys, those brown fruits nestling in their immaculate covering of rosy flick,[6] inspire in me a complex sense of repug-nance that I both seek and repress. But the fine layer of fat that gets left in the hollow of the little forked trotter when the fire cracks open the dead pig's feet, is something I eat gladly, a nour-ishing little delicacy… Never mind. Today, I don't really feel like going with Maman.

My father doesn't insist, but pulls himself deftly up on his single leg, grasps his crutch and his stick and makes his way upstairs to the library. Before going up, he carefully folds his newspaper *Le Temps*, hides it under the cushion of his wing chair, and stuffs *La Nature* with its sky-blue cover into one of the pockets of his long jacket.[7] His small Cossack eye, glittering beneath a brow of grey hemp, sweeps the tables for any printed provender: it will all be taken to the library and never again see the light of day... But we are well practised in this game, and have left nothing for his questing eye to find...

'You haven't seen the *Mercure de France*, have you?'

'No, Papa.'

'Nor the *Revue bleue*?'

'No, Papa.'

He fixes his children with an inquisitorial glare.

'I would dearly like to know who, in this house...'

He gives vent to dark and impersonal conjectures, punctuated by poisonous expletives. His house has become *this* house, where disorder such as *this* reigns, where *these* children, 'basely born', profess their contempt for the written word – and are encouraged to do so, what's more, by *this* woman...

'...And where's that woman got to, by the way?'

'You know, Papa – she's gone to Léonore's!'

'Again!'

'She's only just left...'

He pulls out his watch, winds it up as if he were going up to bed, grabs, for want of anything better, the *Office de Publicité* from the day before yesterday,[8] and goes up to the library. My father's right hand firmly grasps the crossbar·of the crutch that props up his right armpit. The other hand merely avails itself of a stick. I hear this rhythmic thud of two sticks and a single foot – which has lulled my whole childhood – move off at a firm and even pace. But now, today, a new unease troubles me, since

I have suddenly just noticed the prominent veins and wrinkles on my father's strikingly white hands, and how much that fringe of thick hair, on the nape of his neck, has recently lost its colour... Can it really be possible that he'll soon be sixty?...

It's cool and overcast out on the front steps, where I wait for my mother to return. Her elegant little footsteps eventually echo down the rue de la Roche and I am surprised at how happy I feel... She turns the street corner, and makes her way down towards me. Horrid Patasson – the dog – precedes her, and she quickens her pace.

'Don't bother me now, darling – if I don't give Henriette this shoulder of mutton to put in the oven straight away, it'll still be as tough as old boots when we eat it. Where's your father?'

I follow her, vaguely shocked, for the first time, that she should be worried about Papa. Since she left him only half an hour ago and he hardly ever goes out... She knows full well where my father is... She ought rather to have asked me, for instance, 'Little-Darling, you're terribly pasty faced... Little-Darling, what's the matter with you?'

I don't reply, but watch her toss her garden hat away, with a youthful gesture that reveals grey hair and a fresh and ruddy face, albeit one that is marked here and there by deep and permanent furrows. So can it be possible – but of course, I was the last of us four to be born – can it be possible that my mother will soon be fifty-four?... I never think about it. I'd rather forget.

Here he is, the man she was after. Here he is, his hair bristling, his beard jutting out. He was waiting for the front door to slam shut, so that he could come down from his eyrie.

'You back again? Took your time.'

She turns round, quick as a cat.

'Took my time? You're joking, I went straight there and came straight back.'

'Back from where? Léonore's?'

'Oh no, I had to go to Corneau's too, for…'

'For his silly great dunderhead? And his reflections on the weather?'

'Don't be so tiresome! I also went to get some blackcurrant leaves from Cholet's.'

That little Cossack eye darts a piercing glance at her.

'Aha! You went to Cholet's!'

My father flings his head back, runs a hand through his thick, almost white hair.

'Aha, Cholet's, eh? Have you ever noticed that Cholet's hair is falling out? He's as bald as a coot.'

'No, can't say I'd noticed.'

'You hadn't noticed? Oh, so you hadn't noticed! Of course not! You were much too busy making eyes at those lover-boys in the boozer opposite, and the two Mabilat boys!'

'Oh, now you're really going too far! D'you think *I'd* make eyes at the two Mabilat boys? Just you listen to me – I don't know how you can dare… I promise you I never even looked in the direction of Mabilat's house! And to prove it…'

My mother, aflame with anger, crosses her pretty but ageing and weather-beaten hands on her bosom, propped up by a gusseted corset. Her face, framed by her greying hair, blushes, filled with an indignation that makes her dumpy chin tremble: she looks comic, this elderly little lady, when she defends herself, in all seriousness, against a jealous sixty-year-old man. He's perfectly serious too, accusing her as he now does of 'gallivanting around'. But *I* still can't take their quarrels seriously, and they make me laugh, since I'm only fifteen, and still haven't guessed what fierce love lies concealed beneath an old man's eyebrows, or what blushing adolescent feelings can be read on a woman's fading cheeks.

Little One

Over the lush, unmown lawn there lingers a smell of crushed grass, trodden in all directions by children's games that have beaten it down like a heavy hailstorm. Furious little heels have scuffed along the paths, scattering gravel onto the flower beds; a skipping rope is dangling from the pump handle; plates from a doll's dinner service, no bigger than daisies, shine in the grass like stars; a prolonged, bored miaow announces the close of day, the awakening of the cats and the approach of dinner.

Little One's playmates have just this minute left. Disdaining to use the gate, they jumped over the garden railing, flinging into the deserted rue des Vignes their final frenzied shrieks, yelling their childish expletives at the top of their voices, shrugging their shoulders contemptuously, legs astraddle, pulling faces like little toads, going all cross-eyed and sticking out their tongues stained with purple ink. From the other side of the wall, Little One – also known as Little-Darling – sent after them, as they fled, all the raucous laughter she still had in her, all the coarse mockery and local slang. They were rough of speech, those girls, and their cheeks and eyes were as flushed as if someone had got them drunk. Off they went, looking edgy and tired out, as if depraved by a long afternoon devoted entirely to playing games. Neither idle leisure nor boredom ennobled this prolonged and degrading pleasure-seeking, and it has left Little One feeling nauseated and sullied.

Sundays are sometimes days of empty reverie; the white shoes and the starched dress protect us from certain frenzies. But Thursday is a day off, a day for slumming it, for going on strike in our black pinafores and hobnailed boots: on Thursday, everything is permitted. For over five hours, these children have been revelling in the freedom granted them by Thursday. One girl pretended to be poorly, the other sold coffee to a third, a horse dealer, who finally agreed to part with a cow. 'Thirty louis! You've got a bargain there – admit it! Let's shake hands on it!' Jeanne has borrowed old man Gruel's identity as a tripe butcher and tanner of rabbit skins. Yvonne has been taking off Gruel's daughter, a scraggy thing, tormented and dissolute. Scire and his wife, Gruel's neighbours, were accurately impersonated by Gabrielle and Sandrine, and through six childish mouths all the mud of a poor village street flowed in torrents. Scandalous gossip, detailing sordid love affairs and every kind of mischief, curled many a lip that was stained with the blood of cherries and still glistening with the honey from tea-time... A pack of cards was whisked from a pocket, and cries rose into the air. Three little girls already knew how to cheat, wetting their thumbs like the folks in the pub, and slamming the trump card down on the table. 'Trumped it! You've scraped the bottom of the barrel and you still haven't scored a single point!'

They've loudly retold and passionately mimicked all the tittle-tattle you can pick up on village streets. This particular Thursday was one of those that Little-Darling's mother always shuns: she had withdrawn into the house as if filled with fear that an invader were about to break in.

At the moment, everything in the garden is still. One cat, two cats, stretch, yawn and test the gravel with a cautious claw – just as they do after a storm. They pad off towards the house, and Little One, who was trailing after them, stops; she doesn't feel worthy. She is going to wait until her hot face, black with excitement, is slowly illuminated by the pallor of that inner dawn that rises to celebrate the departure of the demons of the underworld. She opens her wide mouth, with its shiny-new front teeth, in one last yell. She stares wide-eyed ahead of her, raises her eyebrows, heaves a 'phew!' of exhaustion, and wipes her nose on the back of her hand.

A school pinafore bags her in from her neck to her knees, and her hair is done in the style of poor children, with two braids tied up behind her ears. What will become of her hands, on which the brambles and the cats have left the traces of their sharp claws? And what about her feet, laced into boots of yellow calfskin? There are days when people say Little One is going to be pretty. Today, she's ugly, and she can sense on her face the provisional ugliness that results from her sweat, the grimy trace of fingers left on her cheek, and above all her gift for mimicry that has made her resemble Jeanne, Sandrine, Aline the daily dressmaker, the chemist's wife and the lady at the post office: the girls' last game was a prolonged bout of 'what-we're-going-to-be-when-we-grow-up'.

'Well, when *I* grows up…'

They're good at aping others, but they lack imagination. A sort of resigned wisdom, the typical villager's terror of adventure and foreign parts, already acts as a check on the clockmaker's daughter and the daughters of the grocer, the butcher and the ironing lady, and keeps them captive in their mothers' shops. Still, there's always Jeanne, who declared, 'I'm going to be a tart!'

'Come off it,' thinks Little-Darling disdainfully, 'that's childish nonsense…'

Unable to come up with a wish, when her turn came, she proclaimed, in a contemptuous tone, 'I'm going to be a sailor!' She does sometimes dream of being a boy and wearing a blue beret and trousers. The sea (which Little-Darling has never seen), the ship rearing up on the crest of a wave, the island bathed in gold with its glowing fruits – all this only came into the picture later on, to serve as a background to the blue jacket and the beret with its pompon.

'I'm going to be a sailor, and in my travels…'

As she sits in the grass, she relaxes and her thoughts grow vacant. Travel? Adventure?… For a girl who crosses the limits of her district only twice a year, on the big winter and spring food-shopping expeditions, and travels to town in a Victoria, these are words with neither force nor virtue. They summon up nothing more than printed pages and coloured pictures. Little One feels tired, and repeats mechanically to herself, 'When I go round the world...' in the same tone of voice as if she were saying, 'When I go shaking the branches for chestnuts...'

A red light gleams in the house, behind the windows of the living room, and Little One shivers. Everything that had been green just a moment ago now turns blue around this motionless red flame. The girl's hand, trailing along through the grass, can feel the damp chill of evening. It's time to light the lamps. A sound like the ripple of running water... it's the leaves rustling; and the door to the hayloft starts to bang against the wall just as it does during a winter squall. The garden is suddenly hostile, and raises its cold laurel leaves against a little girl who has come out of her trance; it lifts its sabres of yucca and the spiky, caterpillar-like branches of its monkey-puzzle trees. An ocean roar comes from the direction of Moutiers where the wind, unhampered by any obstacle, gusts along over the rising swell of the treetops. Little One, in the grass, keeps her eyes fixed on the lamp, which a brief eclipse has just veiled: a hand has passed in front of the flame, a hand with a shining thimble at its fingertip. The movement of this hand is enough for Little One to stand up quickly, growing pale and docile, as she trembles slightly like a child who, for the first time, stops being the cheerful little vampire who unthinkingly drains her mother's heart dry. She trembles slightly at the guilty realisation that the hand and the flame she can see, and that anxious head bent over the lamp, are the secret centre from which – in zones which become ever less perceptible, in circles which the necessary light and vibration fail increasingly to reach – the warm living room emerges, and its flora of cut branches and its fauna of peaceful animals multiply; the echoing house grows dry and crackles like a fresh hot loaf; the garden, the village... Beyond all this, nothing but danger and solitude...

The 'sailor', as she hesitatingly steps forward, tests out terra firma and eventually reaches the house, turning her back on the huge yellow moon as it rises. Adventure? Travel? The pride that drives emigrants?... With her eyes fixed on the shining thimble and on that hand passing back and forth in front of the lamp, Little-Darling revels in the delightful condition of being – just like the clockmaker's daughter, and the daughters of the laundry-woman and the baker – a child of her village, hostile to the coloniser as much as to the barbarian, one of those girls who limit their universe to the edge of a field, the entrance to a shop, the arena of light that falls from a lamp and across which moves a beloved hand as it pulls its thread, its finger tipped by a silver thimble.

The Abduction

'I can't go on living like this,' my mother told me. 'Last night I had another dream about you being abducted. Three times I went up to your bedroom door. And I couldn't get back to sleep.'

I looked at her sympathetically, since she looked tired and worried. And I said nothing, since I couldn't think of anything that would remedy her anxiety.

'Still, you don't seem too bothered, you little monster!'

'Oh Maman!... What am I supposed to say? You seem to think it's my fault that it's only a dream!'

She lifted her arms heavenwards and dashed over to the door, catching the cord of her pince-nez on the key of a drawer and then the gold chain of her lorgnette on the door latch as she swept by, entangling at the same time the sharp, Gothic points on the back of a Second Empire chair in the mesh of her shawl; she suppressed an oath that was about to spring from her lips, and disappeared after an indignant glance at me, murmuring, 'Nine years old she is!... Talking back to me like that, when I want to raise a serious issue!'

My half-sister's marriage had just liberated her bedroom for me, the one on the first storey, with its cornflower-patterned wallpaper like stars on a grey-white background.

Leaving my childhood lair – a small and ancient porter's lodge with huge beams and a tiled floor, perched over the carriage entrance and communicating with my mother's bedroom – I had for a month been sleeping in that bed, which I had never even dared to dream of, that bed from whose rosettes of burnished lead hung white lace curtains with a lining of pitiless blue. This cupboard-closet now belonged to me, and at one or other of its windows I would prop myself up, filled with melancholy and disdain (both feigned) at the times when the little Blancvillain and Trinitet girls were due to pass, biting into their four-o'clock sandwich thickly spread with red haricot beans congealed in a wine sauce. At every opportunity, I would say, 'I'm just popping up to my room… Céline has left the shutters in my room open…'

This happiness was under threat: my mother, filled with anxiety, was on the prowl. Ever since my sister's marriage, she felt she'd lost one of her children. And then there was some story or other about a young girl who'd been abducted and locked away: it was on the front page of all the newspapers. A vagrant, who'd been turned away by our cook as night fell, refused to go away; he stuck his cudgel into the front door, and stayed there until my father arrived… And then, some gypsies I'd met on the road had offered, with glittering smiles and hatred in their eyes, to buy my hair, and M. Demange, that old gentleman who never spoke to anyone, had gone so far as to offer me some sweets from his snuffbox.

'Nothing very serious, then,' my father calmly stated.

'Oh, that's you all over!… So long as nobody interferes with your after-lunch cigarette and your game of dominoes… You've even forgotten that Little One sleeps upstairs now: there's a whole floor, the dining room, the corridor and the living room between her and my bedroom. I've had enough of worrying myself sick over my daughters. Already the eldest has gone off with that fellow…'

'What do you mean, gone off?'

'Well you know, married. And married or not, all the same, she's gone off with a fellow she hardly knows.'

She gazed at my father with affectionate suspicion.

'After all, you know, you're not much to me, are you? You're not even a relative of mine…'

At mealtimes, I would take delight in the stories that were related in veiled terms, couched in that language parents use, in which a hermetic expression replaces a vulgar term, and a meaningful glance and shrug, accompanied by a dramatic 'Ahem!', attract and sustain the children's attention.

'In Ghent, when I was a girl,' my mother would say, 'one of my friends, who was only sixteen, was abducted... She really was! And in a two-horse carriage, what's more! The next day... Ahem!... Of course. There could be no question of handing her back to her family. Once – how shall I put it? – once the premises had been burgled... Anyway, they finally got married. There was nothing for it.'

'There was nothing for it!'

Not a very sensible thing to say... A small, ancient engraving, in the darkness of the corridor, suddenly aroused my interest. It depicted a post-chaise, harnessed to two strange horses with necks like those of monstrous beasts. Just in front of the gaping carriage door, a young man dressed in taffeta was carrying in one arm, with the greatest of ease, a young girl who was fainting away, while her little round lips opening in an O, and her skirts frilled out like a rumpled corolla around two rather attractive legs endeavoured to express the full horror of the situation. '*The Abduction!*' My innocent daydreams caressed both the word and the image...

One windy night when the farmyard doors hadn't been closed properly and kept banging, and above me the loft was groaning, swept by gust after gust of wind sweeping in from west to east and slipping under the edges of the badly fitting slates, where it blew clear melodies, as if on a harmonica, I was asleep, completely exhausted by a Thursday spent out in the fields shaking down chestnuts from their branches and celebrating the brewing of the new cider. Did I dream that my door was creaking? So many hinges, so many weathercocks creaking and groaning all around... Two arms, well-practised in the art of lifting up a sleeping body, then enfolded my waist and neck, simultaneously pressing the blanket and the sheet around me.

My cheek perceived the cooler air of the staircase; someone walked downstairs with a slow, heavy, muffled tread, and each step rocked me gently. Did I fully wake up? I doubt it. Only a dream can sweep a little girl up from her childhood with a single beat of its wings, and set her down, neither surprised nor rebellious, in the midst of her hypocritical and adventurous adolescence. Only a dream can metamorphose a tender-hearted child into the ungrateful person she will be tomorrow: the stranger's sly accomplice, the forgetful woman who will leave the maternal household without even looking round... And so I left for the land where the post-chaise, its bronze bells jingling, stops outside the church and sets down a young man in taffeta and a young girl who, in the disorder of her skirts, looks like a rose with dishevelled petals... I did not cry out. The two arms treated me so gently, and took such care to hold me tight, to make sure my dangling feet did not bump into the doors as we passed by... Yes, a familiar rhythm lulled me to sleep in those ravishing arms...

At daybreak, I did not recognise my old garret, now encumbered with ladders and rickety furniture, where my mother had with great difficulty carried me during the night, like a mother cat secretly moving her kitten from one sleeping place to another. She was asleep, tired out, and she awoke only when my shrill wail rose to the walls of my abandoned porter's lodge: 'Maman! Come quick! I've been abducted!'

The Priest on the Wall

'What are you thinking about, Bel-Gazou?'

'Nothing, Maman.'

A good answer. I always gave the same answer when I was her age. I was called 'Bel-Gazou', just as my daughter is by friends and family. Where does 'Bel-Gazou' come from, and why did my father call me by this name? It's a local term from Provence, no doubt – '*beau gazouillis*', pleasant twittering, pleasant language – but it wouldn't be out of place if applied to the hero or heroine of a Persian fairy tale…

'Nothing, Maman.' It's no bad thing for children, from time to time, to politely put their parents in their place. All temples are sacred. How interfering and heavy-handed I must seem to my own Bel-Gazou just now! My question drops like a stone and shatters the magic mirror that reflects the image of a girl whom I will never know, surrounded by her favourite phantoms. I'm aware that for her father, my daughter is a kind of young female paladin who reigns over her domains, brandishes a lance made from a hazel switch, cleaves the haycocks and urges on her flock before her as though she were taking it on a crusade. I know that a smile from her fills him with delight, and that when he murmurs, 'Right now, she looks adorable,' it is because at that moment, a young girl's tender face suddenly bears an uncanny resemblance to a certain man's face…

I know that, to her faithful nurse, my Bel-Gazou is, in turn, the centre of the world, a consummate masterpiece, a monster in thrall to diabolical possession from whom at every hour the demon must be driven out, a champion runner, a dizzying abyss of perversity, a *dear little one*[9] and a little bunny rabbit… But who can tell me how my daughter appears in her own eyes?

At her age – not quite eight – I was the priest on a wall. This was the high, thick wall that separated the garden from the farmyard, whose summit, as broad as a pavement, lined by flat tiles, served me as a racecourse and a terrace, inaccessible to the ordinary run of mortals. Oh yes: a priest on a wall. What's so incredible about that? I was a priest without liturgical obligations to observe or sermons to deliver: I didn't indulge in any irreverent cross-dressing but, unbeknownst to anyone, I was a very reverend Reverend, just as you are bald, sir, or you, madam, arthritic.

The word 'presbytery' had, that year, happened to fall into my attentive ear, where it wreaked havoc.

'It's certainly the most cheerful presbytery that I know...' someone had said.

Nothing was further from my mind than the idea of asking either of my parents, 'What's a presbytery?' I had taken the mysterious word into myself: the start of the word stood out like a piece of coarse embroidery, and it had a long-drawn-out, dreamy final syllable...[10] Bearing the treasure of my secret and my doubt, I would doze off to sleep with the *word* and hoist it up with me onto my wall. 'Presbytery!' I would fling it, across the roof of the hen-house and Miton's garden, towards the horizon of Moutiers, forever swathed in mist. From the top of my wall, the word rang out like an anathema. 'Begone! You are all presbyteries!' I would shout to invisible outlaws being sent into exile.

Shortly afterwards, the word lost some of its venom, and I realised that 'presbytery' might well be the scientific name of a certain little yellow-and-black-striped snail... A careless remark was my ruin: it was one of those occasions when a child, however serious or however whimsical she might be, bears a fleeting resemblance to the idea that grown-ups have of her...

'Maman! Look at the lovely little presbytery I've found!'

'The lovely little... what?'

'The lovely little presb...'

I stopped, too late. I had to learn ('I sometimes wonder if that child's quite all there...') the things that I'd really rather not have known, and call a spade a spade...

'But a presbytery is the house where a priest lives.'

'The house where a priest lives... So Father Millot lives in a presbytery?'

'Of course... Close your mouth, breathe through your nose... Of course, you know he does.'

I still tried to react... I fought against this unwelcome irruption, and hugged to myself the rags and tatters of my eccentric ideas; I was filled with the desire to force Father Millot to live, at my pleasure, in the empty shell of the little snail known as a 'presbytery'...

'Will you please get into the habit of keeping your mouth closed when you're not speaking? What are you thinking about?'

'Nothing, Maman...'

...And then I gave in. I suddenly succumbed to a fit of cowardice, and I compromised with my disappointment. I chucked away the fragments of the crushed little snail, and picked up the lovely word; I climbed back onto my narrow terrace in the shade of the old lilacs, decorated with polished pebbles and bits of coloured glass like a thieving magpie's nest, and baptised the place 'Presbytery'; and here I ordained myself priest on the wall.

My Mother and Books

The lamp shone through the top of the lampshade and lit up a wall that was corrugated with the spines of bound books. The opposite wall was yellow, the dirty yellow of the covers of paperbacks read, reread, dog-eared. Some were 'translated from English' – one franc twenty-five – and these filled the lower shelf with a dash of red.

Halfway up, Musset, Voltaire, and the Four Gospels[11] gleamed from under their dead-leaf-coloured sheepskin covers. Littré, Larousse and Becquerel arched their backs like so many black tortoises.[12] D'Orbigny,[13] pulled to pieces by the irreverent worship of four children, displayed a scatter of pages emblazoned with dahlias, parrots, jellyfish with pink fringes, and duck-billed platypuses.

Camille Flammarion,[14] in blue with gold stars, contained the yellow planets, the cold, chalk-white craters of the moon, and Saturn rolling through space like an iridescent pearl, floating free within its ring...

Two solid boards as brown as the soil bound the pages of Élisée Reclus.[15] Musset, Voltaire, both mottled, Balzac in black and Shakespeare in olive green...

I need only to shut my eyes and, after so many years, I can again see that book-lined room. In bygone days, I could make them out even in the dark. I didn't need to take a lamp to choose one of them when evening fell: I simply needed to tap along the shelves with my fingertips. They are now destroyed, lost or stolen, but I can still count them all. Almost all of them had witnessed my birth.

There was a time when, before I knew how to read, I would curl up between two volumes of the Larousse like a dog in its kennel. Labiche and Daudet soon inveigled themselves into my happy childhood, like condescending masters playing with a familiar pupil.[16] Mérimée arrived at the same time, seductive and severe, sometimes dazzling the eight-year-old girl I was with a light beyond my understanding.[17] *Les Misérables* too, yes, *Les Misérables*, in spite of Gavroche;[18] but here I'm talking of a rather calculating passion, which experienced periods of coolness and even prolonged indifference. There was no love lost between Dumas and me, although *The Queen's Necklace* filled my dreams for several nights as it sparkled around the doomed neck of Jeanne de la Motte. Neither the enthusiasm of my brothers, nor the surprise and disapproval of my parents, managed to persuade me to take any interest in the Musketeers…[19]

As for children's books, there was never any question of them. I was in love with the Princess in her chariot, dreaming the time away under such a slender crescent moon, and of Sleeping Beauty in her wood, lying prostrate between her pageboys; I had fallen for Lord Puss in his great funnel boots, and I tried to find in Perrault's text the velvety blacks, the gleam of silver, the ruins, the knights, the dainty hooves of the horses depicted by Gustave Doré; after two pages, I returned, in disappointment, to Doré.[20] Only in Walter Crane's fresh illustrations could I read the adventure of the Hind, or of Beauty.[21] The large characters of the text joined one picture to the next just as the unadorned stretches of tulle join the separate decorative motifs in a piece of lace. Not a word ever crossed the threshold that I locked and bolted against them. What happens, later on, to that intense desire *not* to know, that tranquil strength we deploy to banish things and keep them far from us?…

Books, books, books… It wasn't as if I read all that many. I read and reread the same ones. But they were all necessary to me. Their presence, their smell, the letters of their titles and the grain of their leather binding… And as for the most hermetic of them, weren't they the ones that were dearest to me? I forgot the name of the author of a certain Encyclopedia clad in red long ago, but the alphabetical references indicated on each volume cannot fail to compose a magical word: *Aphbicécladiggalhy-maroidphoreb-stevanzy*. How much I liked Guizot, arrayed in all his green and gold but never opened![22] And the *Travels of Anacharsis*, still inviolate![23] If the *History of the Consulate and the Empire* ever ended up on the *quais*, I'll bet a label proudly pointed out its 'condition as new'…[24]

The eighteen volumes of Saint-Simon would in turn find their way to my mother's bedside table night after night; she derived ever-new joys from them, and she was amazed that at the age of eight I didn't share her pleasure.[25]

'Why don't you read Saint-Simon?' she would ask me. 'It's so odd to see how long it takes children to pick up on interesting books!'

Good books that I did read, good books that I didn't read; the warm lining of the walls of my home, the tapestry whose hidden motley delighted my expert eyes… Here it was that I learnt, long before the age of love, that love is complicated and tyrannical and even rather burdensome, since my mother begrudged the place it occupied in all those stories.

'It's a bit of a bore, all those love affairs you get in books,' she used to say. 'My poor Little-Darling, people have other fish to fry in real life. So all those lovesick characters you find in books – don't they ever have children to bring up, or gardens to look after? Little-Darling, you be judge: have you and your brothers ever heard me harping on about love the way they do in books? And yet I know a thing or two about it, it seems to me – I've had two husbands and four children!'

The alluring abysses of fear that yawned in so many novels swarmed, if I leant over them, with quite enough classically white ghosts, sorcerers, shadows, and malevolent beasts, but this supernatural realm did not cling to my dangling plaits and try to climb up to me: it was held at bay by a few magic spells…

'Did you read that ghost story, Little-Darling? It's lovely, isn't it? Is there anything lovelier than that page when the ghost is walking abroad at midnight, through the moonlit cemetery? When the author says, you know, that the light of the moon passed right through the ghost and it didn't cast any shadow on the grass… It must be a wonderful sight, a ghost. I'd love to see one; I'd call you if I did. Sadly, ghosts don't exist. If I could turn myself into a ghost after my life, I wouldn't hesitate to do so – for your pleasure and mine. Did you also read that stupid story about a dead woman taking her revenge? Revenge – I ask you! It would hardly be worth dying if we didn't become more sensible than we'd been before. The dead… well, they're nice, quiet neighbours. My living neighbours don't give me any grief, and I'll take good care that I never get any from my dead neighbours!'

A certain coolness towards literature – quite a healthy attitude, all things considered – preserved me from getting too worked up about novels, and led me (a little later, when I came up against certain books whose tried-and-tested power was supposedly infallible) to keep a critical distance when I should have just surrendered like an intoxicated victim. Was I still imitating my mother, whose peculiar innocence inclined her to deny the existence of Evil, even though her curiosity sought it out and contemplated it in wonder, all jumbled up as it was with Good?

'This one? It's not such a bad book, Little-Darling,' she would tell me. 'Yes, I know, there's that one scene, that one chapter… But it's a novel. Writers run out of ideas, you know, always have done. You should have waited a year or two before reading it… Ah well, have a go and see how you get on, Little-Darling. You're bright enough to keep it to yourself if you understand a bit too much… And perhaps there's no such thing as a bad book…'

There were, however, those books that my father kept locked away in his thuja-wood desk. But it was the author's name that he was most concerned to lock away.

'I don't see what use it is for the children to read Zola!'

Zola bored him, and rather than seeking in this a reason for allowing or forbidding us to read him, he placed on the Index[26] a huge complete edition of Zola that was periodically swelled by further yellow alluvial deposits.[27]

'Maman, why can't I read Zola?'

Those grey eyes, which found it so difficult to lie, betrayed their perplexity.

'Obviously, I'd prefer you not to read certain books by Zola…'

'So why not give me the ones that aren't "certain books"?'

She gave me *The Sin of Father Mouret* and *Doctor Pascal*, and *Germinal*. But I wanted, feeling wounded to discover that there was a corner of this house which had been locked and sealed against me, even though all doors were open, the cats could come in at night, and the cellar and the butter dish were always being mysteriously emptied – I wanted the others. I got them. Even if she later feels ashamed, a fourteen-year-old girl finds it neither difficult nor praiseworthy to deceive her pure-hearted parents. I went off into the garden with my first stolen book. It contained – like several other books by Zola – a rather mawkish story about heredity. The robust and kindly cousin yielded her beloved cousin to a sickly female friend, and, well, it would all have ended up exactly as in a story by Ohnet[28] if the ailing wife hadn't had the joy of bringing a child into the world. She gave birth suddenly, with a rough-and-ready, crude wealth of detail, an anatomical precision, and a lingering over colours, postures and cries, in which I recognised none of the tranquil, knowing experience on which I as a country girl could draw. I felt credulous, startled and vulnerable in my nascent femininity… The matings of grazing beasts, tomcats covering she-cats like wild beasts leaping on their prey, and the peasant-like, almost austere precision of farmers' wives talking about their virginal heifer or their daughter's labour pains – I summoned you all to my aid. But above all I summoned the voice of exorcism:

'When I gave birth to you – you were the last, Little-Darling – I was in pain for three days and two nights. While I was carrying you, I was the size of a house. Three days seem a long time… The animals put us women to shame – we've forgotten how to give birth joyfully. But I've never regretted the pain I went through: people say that children who are carried so high in the womb and take so long to come down towards the light are always deeply loved children, since they have chosen to lie right next to their mother's heart, and are reluctant to leave it…'

In vain I wanted these sweet, hastily assembled words of exorcism to sing in my ears: a silvery buzz deafened me. Other words, right in front of my eyes, depicted flesh splitting open, excrement and sullied blood… I managed to look up, and saw that the blue-hued garden and the smoke-coloured walls were wavering strangely under a sky that had turned yellow… The lawn rose to welcome me, and I toppled head-first, limp like one of those little hares that poachers sometimes brought, freshly killed, into the kitchen.

When I regained consciousness, the sky was once more bright blue, and I was lying at my mother's feet, breathing deeply, my nose rubbed with eau de Cologne.

'Feeling better, Little-Darling?'

'Yes… I don't know what came over me…'

Those grey eyes, gradually looking less worried, fixed their gaze on mine.

'*I* know what it was… A sharp little tap on the head from the hand of God…'

I lay there, pale and dejected, and my mother misinterpreted me.

'It's all right, just forget about it... It's not so terrible, you know, the arrival of a child. And it's much more wonderful in reality. The pain it causes is soon forgotten – you'll see!... The proof that all women forget it is that it's only ever men – and what business was it of old Zola, anyway? – who go into grisly detail about it...'

Propaganda

When I turned eight, nine, ten years old, my father developed an interest in politics. He was a born charmer and fighter, a good improviser and raconteur; later on, I reflected that he might well have been a successful politician, able to enthral Parliament the same way that he seduced a woman. But just as his boundless generosity was the ruin of us all, his childish confidence blinded him. He believed in the sincerity of his supporters and the decency of his adversary – in the shape of M. Merlou. It was M. Pierre Merlou, later a here-today-gone-tomorrow minister, who ousted my father from the general council and prevented him from standing as a *député*. Thank goodness for His late lamented Excellency!

A job heading a small tax-collector's office in the Yonne wasn't enough to keep someone like him quiet and docile: a captain of the Zouaves who'd lost a leg, he was as fiery as gunpowder and afflicted by philanthropic views. As soon as the word 'politics' started to make a din in his ears like the pernicious rattle of sabres, he thought, 'I will win over the people by educating them; I will spread the word to children and young people, instructing them in the sacred names of natural history and elementary physics and chemistry, I will go forth, brandishing the magic lantern and the microscope, and distributing in every village school educational and eye-catching coloured plates in which the weevil, magnified twenty times life-size, humiliates the vulture, who is reduced to the size of a bee… I will lecture to the public on the dangers of alcohol, and those who dwell in Puisaye and Forterre, habitual and hardened drinkers though they be, shall be converted by my words and depart washed clean by their floods of tears!…'

He did as he had planned. When the time came, the shabby old Victoria and the aged black mare were loaded with the magic lantern, painted diagrams, test tubes, bent pipes, the prospective candidate, his crutches, and me: it was a clear, cold autumn day, with a pale blue cloudless sky, the mare slowed to a walk each time we went up a hill, and I would leap to the ground to pick blue sloes and coral-coloured spindle-berries from the hedgerows, and to gather white mushrooms, all rosy in their conches like seashells. From the almost bare woods that we passed there emerged a sweet aroma of fresh truffles and rain-soaked leaves.

Life became very pleasant for me just then. In the villages, the schoolroom, emptied an hour previously, welcomed listeners to its worn-down benches; I recognised the blackboard, the weights and measures and the sour odour of dirty children. A petrol lamp, swinging on its chain, illuminated the faces of those who came along, mistrustful and unsmiling, to hear the good news. The effort of listening made their brows wrinkle, and their mouths fell open like those of martyrs. But I sat apart from them, aloof on the podium, fulfilling more serious duties, and savouring the pride that swells the young stage assistant whose job it is to present the juggler with his plaster eggs, silk scarf and blue-bladed daggers.

The end of the 'highly instructive talk' was greeted by a perplexed torpor, and then a timid round of applause. A mayor with clogs on his feet congratulated my father as if he had just escaped a shameful conviction. On the threshold of the empty room, children waited for the 'man with one leg' to pass by. The cold night air clung to my flushed face like a wet handkerchief soaked in the powerful, steamy aroma of new-ploughed fields, cowsheds and the bark of oak trees. The harnessed mare, black in the black night, whinnied at us, and in the halo of one of the lamps turned the horned shadow of her head… But my father, magnificent in hospitality, would not leave his dour disciples without offering a round of drinks to – at the very least – the members of the town council. At the nearest 'watering hole' the hot wine would be bubbling on the living embers, with bits of lemon rind and shreds of cinnamon bobbing about on its empurpled swell. Whenever I think of it, the heady steam it gave off moistens my nostrils all over again… As a good Southerner, my father would only ever take a glass of 'sparkling', whereas his daughter…

'This young lady's going to warm herself up with a drop of hot wine!'

A drop? If the café proprietor took away the spout of the jug too quickly, I knew how to order, 'Fill her up!', adding 'Cheers!', before clinking glasses, lifting my elbow, and banging the bottom of my empty glass on the table; then I would wipe away the moustache stain of mulled burgundy with the back of my hand, pushing my glass towards the wine jug. 'That goes down a treat, that does!' Oh, I knew how to behave all right!

My rural courtesy made the drinkers relax: now they suddenly caught a glimpse of my father as a man just like them – apart from his amputated leg – who 'speaks well, though maybe he is a bit of a crackpot'… The session which had begun as a chore ended in back-slapping laughter, in tall stories barked out by raucous voices as hoarse as a sheepdog who sleeps out all seasons… I would doze off to sleep, completely drunk, my head on the table, lulled by this benevolent tumult. Brawny ploughmen's arms would eventually pick me up and deposit me in the back of the carriage, tenderly, having first wrapped round me the red tartan shawl that smelled of orris root[29] and Maman…

Ten kilometres, sometimes fifteen, a real journey beneath the breathless stars of a winter sky, and the mare trotting along with her belly full of oats… Are there people who remain indifferent, who are never affected by a lump in the throat or a childlike sob, when they hear, on a road hard and dry with frost, the trot of a horse, the yelp of a hunting fox, the hoot of an owl blinded by the harsh light of the passing lamps?...

The first few times, on our return, my blissful prostration filled my mother with amazement. She quickly put me to bed, and ticked my father off for letting me get over-tired. Then one evening she noticed that my eyes were filled with a very Burgundian type of merriment, and smelt on my breath the secret cause of my merry banter – alas!...

The Victoria left without me the next day, returned that evening and never left again.

'Have you given up your lectures?' my mother asked my father, a few days later.

He glanced quickly at me with a melancholy and flattering expression in his eyes, and shrugged.

'Damn it! You've taken my best electoral agent from me!'

Papa and Madame Bruneau

Nine o'clock, summer, a garden that seems larger in the evening, the period of rest before sleep. Hurried footsteps crunch along the gravel, between the terrace and the pump, between the pump and the kitchen. Sitting close to the ground on a little footstool that is hard and uncomfortable, I lean my head, as I do every evening, on my mother's knees, and I make a guess with my eyes closed: 'That's the heavy tread of Morin, he's just been watering the tomatoes... That's the tread of Mélie who's off to empty the potato parings... The light tread of high heels: that's Madame Bruneau who's coming for a chat with Maman...'
An attractive voice comes down to me from above:

'Little-Darling, why don't you say "good evening" nicely to Mme Bruneau?'

'She's half asleep, leave her alone, poor little thing...'

'Little-Darling, if you are asleep, you should go up to bed.'

'Can't I stay a bit longer, Maman, just a bit? I don't feel sleepy...'

A slender hand, with the three little calluses I cherish, the product of the rake, the secateurs and the dibble, smooths down my hair and pinches my ear:

'I know, I know that eight-year-old children never get sleepy.'

I stay there in the dark, against Maman's knees. Without going to sleep, I close my useless eyes. The linen dress to which I press my cheek smells of plain soap, the wax used to polish the irons, and violets. I have only to move slightly away from this gardener's dress with its fresh fragrance, and my head immediately plunges into a haze of perfume that washes over us like a great smooth wave: the white tobacco plant opens to the night its narrow tubes of fragrance and its star-shaped corollas. A ray of light touches the walnut tree and awakens it: it makes a sound like lapping water, stirred down to its lowest branches by a slender oar of moonlight. The wind superimposes onto the odour of white tobacco the bitter, chill odour of the little worm-eaten walnuts that tumble onto the lawn.

The ray of moonlight shines down onto the flags of the terrace, where it rouses a velvety baritone voice – my father's. The voice sings 'Pageboy, squire and captain'. It will doubtless go on to sing:

> *I think of you, I see you, I adore you,*
> *At every moment, everywhere, always…*

unless (since Mme Bruneau likes sad music) it launches into:

> *Weary of combat, thus did he sing,*
> *On the icy banks of Dnieper the grim…*

But this evening, it is more nuanced and inflected, and goes so deep it makes you shudder, filling you with nostalgia for the time…

> *When the lovely queen forgot*
> *The crown on her head for her pageboy sweet,*
> *To whom she'd lost her heart!*

'The Captain has such a voice, he should really be on stage,' Mme Bruneau sighs.

'If he'd only wanted to…' replies Maman, full of pride. 'He's so gifted.'

The ray of the rising moon strikes the silhouette of a man standing bolt upright on the terrace, one hand – so white that it looks green – gripping a bar of the railing. His crutch and his cane, flung aside disdainfully, lean against the wall. My father rests like a heron on his single leg, and sings.

'Ah!' Mme Bruneau sighs again, 'each time I hear the Captain sing, it makes me sad. You have no idea what a life like mine is like… Growing old beside a husband like my poor husband… Telling myself I'll never have known love…'

'Mme Bruneau,' that stirring voice breaks in, 'you do know that my offer still stands?'

I hear Mme Bruneau give a start in the shadows, and her feet scrape the gravel:

'The villain! The villain! Captain, you'll make me run away!'

'Forty sous and a packet of tobacco,' the voice imperturbably pursues. 'I wouldn't make such an offer to anyone else. Forty sous and a packet of tobacco to teach you the meaning of love – do you think the price is too high? Mme Bruneau, don't be stingy! The minute I put up my rates, you'll regret you didn't take me up on my present terms: forty sous and a packet of tobacco…'

I hear Mme Bruneau's scandalised protestations as she takes flight: a plump, flabby little woman, her temples already grey. I hear my mother's indulgent rebukes – she always calls her husband by our family name:

'Oh, Colette!… Colette!…'

My father's voice launches another couple of lines of song at the moon; and little by little I cease to hear him. As I sleep between my mother's knees, which she has positioned to ensure I'll be comfy, I forget all about Mme Bruneau and the bawdy teasings that she comes here to seek on evenings when the weather is fine…

But on the following day, and on all the succeeding days, however much our neighbour, Mme Bruneau, stays on the alert, peering every way before scuttling across the road as if she were dodging the spots of a shower, she cannot escape her enemy – her idol.

Standing erect and proud on one leg, or else sitting and rolling his cigarette in one hand, or embastioned treacherously behind the unfolded pages of his *Le Temps*: there he is. She can run by, holding up her skirt in both hands as if in a quadrille, or she can noiselessly slip along the walls of the houses, sheltered under her purple parasol, but he'll always shout after her, in a light-hearted, engaging tone:

'Forty sous and a packet of tobacco!'

There are souls capable of concealing their wounds for a long time, and the quiver of temptation they feel at the idea of sin. This is what Mme Bruneau did. She put up with the scandalous offer and the cynical nods and winks as much as she could, and tried to turn them into a joke. Then, one day, leaving her little house behind, and taking her furniture and her derisory husband with her, she moved, and went off to live far, far away from us, up there in the hills of Bel-Air.

My brother shrugged.

'You can't understand, you're only seven. Put the strong glue in the bain-marie. And make up two little wreaths of blue beads for the tomb of the Azioume twins, they were born and died on the same day.'

'Oh!... Were they nice?'

'Very nice,' said my brother. 'Two boys, blond hair, completely alike. I'm doing something a bit different for them: two broken columns in rolled cardboard. I'll paint them to look like marble, and then stick the bead wreaths round them. Oh yes, old girl!...'

He whistled in admiration and continued his work in silence. Around him, the granary was blossoming with little white tombs: it was a cemetery for big dolls. This eccentric hobby of his involved no irreverent parody, no macabre display. He had never knotted the strings of an apron under his chin to mimic a chasuble as he sang the *Dies Irae*. But he loved cemeteries in the same way that other people love formal gardens, ornamental ponds or kitchen gardens. He would set off with his usual fleetness of foot to visit all the village cemeteries within a circumference of fifteen kilometres, and then tell me all about his explorations.

'At Escamps, old girl, it's really stylish, there's a notary there buried in a chapel as big as the gardener's shed, with a glass door – you can see an altar through it, some flowers, a cushion lying on the ground and a tapestry chair.'

'A chair? Who for?'

'For the dead man, I think, when he comes back at night.'

From his earliest childhood, he had preserved that gently eccentric attitude, that inoffensive wildness that protects very young children from the fear of death and bloodshed. At the age of thirteen, he didn't really distinguish between a living person and a dead one. While my own games brought into being before

53

My Mother and Animals

A series of brutal noises, the train, the cabs, the buses – that's all my memory can still tell me of a short stay in Paris when I was six. Five years later, all I can recall of a week in Paris is a memory of dry heat, panting thirst, feverish fatigue and the fleas in a hotel room in the rue Saint-Roch. I can also remember that I kept looking up, feeling vaguely oppressed by the height of the houses, and that a photographer won me over by calling me, as I think he called every child, a 'wonder'. Five years in the provinces elapsed, and I hardly thought about Paris.

But at the age of sixteen, coming back to Puisaye after a fort-night of theatres, museums and shops, I brought home with me – among memories of flirtation and gluttony mingled with regrets, hopes and scorns as intense, innocent and ungainly as I was myself – a sense of amazement and a melancholy aversion towards what I called all the 'houses without animals'. Those cubes without gardens, those dwellings without flowers, where no cats miaow from behind the dining-room door, where you never step onto some part of a dog's body as it slouches near the fire like a carpet, those apartments deprived of familiar spirits, where your hand, seeking a friendly caress, merely encounters inanimate marble, wood or velvet: when I left them, my senses were still hungry, and I felt a vehement need to touch living things – animals' coats, leaves, warm feathers, the poignant moistness of flowers...

As if I were discovering them all at the same time, I greeted, as if they formed one inseparable entity, my mother, the garden and our circle of animals. The hour of my return came just as the garden was being watered, and I still cherish that sixth hour of the evening, the green watering can that soaked the blue sateen dress, the sharp odour of the humus, the declining light that fastened its pink glow onto the white page of a forgotten book,

onto the white corollas of the white tobacco plant, onto the white patch of the cat's fur in her basket.

Nonoche the tortoiseshell had given birth to kittens two days previously, and Bijou, her daughter, the following night; as for Musette, the Havanese bitch, her production of bastards was unstoppable...

'Little-Darling, go and take a look at Musette's puppy!'

I went off to the kitchen: and there indeed lay Musette, feeding a monster with an ashen-grey coat, still almost blind, nearly as big as she was, the son of a hunting dog, tugging like a calf at her delicate teats all strawberry pink in the silvery fur, and trampling rhythmically with its sharp claws a silky belly that it would have torn unless... unless my mother hadn't cut out and sewn for it, out of an ancient pair of white gloves, some little suede mittens that came up to its elbows. I've never seen a ten-day-old puppy looking so much like a gendarme.

How many treasures had blossomed in my absence! I rushed to the huge basket overflowing with indistinct cats. That orange ear belonged to Nonoche. But whose was this plume of a black, angora tail? It could belong only to Bijou, her daughter, as intolerant as a pretty woman. A long paw, slender and dry, like the paw of a black rabbit, threatened the heavens; a tiny little cat, spotted like a genet, lay sleeping, replete, belly upwards amid all this disorder, looking as if it had been murdered... Filled with happiness, I sorted out these nursing mothers and their well-licked nurslings, fragrant with hay and fresh milk and well-tended fur, and I discovered that Bijou, four times a mother in three years, bringing to her teats a chaplet of newborns, was herself sucking, with the clumsy noise of her over-large tongue and the purring of a chimney fire, the milk of old Nonoche lying inertly there, taking her ease with one paw over her eyes.

I bent to listen to the double purring, one grave and the other silvery, that mysterious privilege of the cat family – the rumble

of a distant factory, the buzz of an imprisoned coleopteran, a delicate mill which falls into a deep sleep and brings the mill-wheel to a halt. I wasn't surprised to see this chain of cats suckling one another. Anybody who lives in the fields and uses his or her eyes finds that everything soon seems miraculous and simple. We had long since viewed it as perfectly natural for a hound bitch to feed a kitten, for a female cat to choose as her sleeping place the top of a cage in which trusting green canaries sang, sometimes using their beaks to pull out a few silky hairs from the sleeping animal to adorn their nests.

A whole year of my childhood was devoted to capturing the rare winter flies in the kitchen or the cowshed, so as to feed them to two swallows – an October brood blown down by the wind. Surely it was my duty to save those insatiable creatures with their gaping beaks, who disdained to eat dead meat? It's thanks to them that I know how much the tame swallow surpasses the most spoilt dog in insolent sociability. Our two swallows lived perched on our shoulders, or on our heads, or nestled in the work-basket, darting under the table like hens and pecking the dog, who was dumbfounded, or chirruping into the face of the cat, who was completely taken aback… They came to school in my pocket, and winged their way back home. When the shining sickle of their wings grew long and sharp, they vanished into the depths of the spring sky at every hour of the day, but a single shrill cry, 'Hey…! Little biiiiiirdies…!' brought them back, cleaving the wind like two swift arrows, and they would land in my hair, clinging as tightly as they could with their curved claws shining like black steel.

How enchanted and simple life was in the midst of the fauna of my home… You didn't know that a cat could eat straw-berries? But *I* know it can: I saw it happen so many times – how that black Satan, Babou, his body as endless and sinuous as an eel, would, with all the good taste of a real gourmet, choose from

Mme Pomié's kitchen garden the ripest of strawberries, both the royal sovereign variety and the early scarlets. It was the same creature who would sniff, with a poetic air of absorption, the newly opened violets. You've heard the story of Pellisson's music-loving spider?[30] It comes as no surprise to me. But I'll add my own slender contribution to the treasure-house of human knowledge, and just mention the spider that, according to Papa, my mother had on her ceiling, that same year that I celebrated my sixteenth birthday. A fine garden spider she was too, with its belly shaped like a clove of garlic, emblazoned with a storiated cross. She would sleep or go hunting, during the day, on her web that hung from the bedroom ceiling. At night, around three o'clock, just as my mother's regular bouts of insomnia relit the lamp and reopened the book on the bedside table, the big spider would also wake up, make a careful survey of the lie of the land, and lower herself from the ceiling dangling from a thread, right over the little oil lamp where a bowl of chocolate simmered gently all night long. Down she came, slowly, swaying gently like a great pearl, grabbing onto the edge of the cup with her eight legs, leaning forward and drinking until she was full. Then up again she would go, heavy with creamy chocolate, making all the halts and pauses for reflection that an over-full stomach rendered necessary, and reassuming her position in the centre of her silken rigging…

Still enwrapped in my travelling coat, I would dream, weary but enchanted, quite won over, my rediscovered kingdom all around me.

'Where's your spider, Maman?'

My mother's grey eyes, magnified by her glasses, grew sad.

'So you've come all the way back from Paris, and all you can ask about is my spider? Ungrateful girl!'

I hung my head, inept in love, ashamed of what was most pure within me.

'At night, when I couldn't get to sleep, I'd sometimes think of those times when the spider appears…'

'Little-Darling, did you have difficulty sleeping? Hadn't they given you a comfortable bed?… The spider's in her web, I imagine. But come and see if my caterpillar is asleep. I think she's just about to turn into a chrysalis – I've given her a little box with dry sand in it. She's the caterpillar of an emperor moth: a bird must have given her a bit of a peck on the stomach, but she's better now…'

The caterpillar was perhaps asleep, moulding her form to the curve of a branch of tea-plant. The ravages she had made all around attested to her strength: nothing left but shreds of leaves, gnawed stems, and shoots sucked dry. Plump and round as a thumb, over ten centimetres long, she arched the swelling fat rolls of her cabbage-green body, studded with prominent, hairy turquoises. I gently pulled her off and she writhed in anger, showing her paler underbelly and all her spiky little paws clinging like so many suckers to the branch where I set her down again.

'Maman, she's gobbled it all up!'

Those grey eyes behind her glasses turned their gaze from the denuded tea-plant to the caterpillar, and from the caterpillar to me, looking puzzled.

'Well, I don't think there's much I can do about that, is there? Anyway, the tea-plant she eats, you know, is the same tea-plant that chokes the honeysuckle…'

'But the caterpillar can eat honeysuckle too…'

'I don't know… Anyway, what do you expect me to do about it? After all, I can hardly kill the poor creature…'

It's still there, right in front of my eyes: the garden with its warm walls, the last dark cherries hanging from the tree, the sky webbed with long pink clouds – it's all still there at my finger-tips: the caterpillar wriggling vigorously and rebelliously, the

thick, moist leather of the hydrangea leaves – and my mother's callused little hand. If I so desire, the wind rustles the stiff paper of the false bamboo, as the combs of the yew-branches divide the breeze into a thousand streams of air, sings along in worthy accompaniment to the voice that, on that day and every other day until the final silence, words that never varied very much, but said:

'Someone needs to keep an eye on that child... Can't anyone save that woman? Have those people got enough to eat at home? After all, I really can't kill that creature...'

Epitaphs

'What did he do then, when he was alive, that Astoniphronque Bonscop?'

My brother[31] threw back his head, clasped his hands round his knee, and narrowed his eyes the better to see, at a distance inaccessible to coarse human vision, the forgotten features of Astoniphronque Bonscop.

'He was the town crier. But at home he repaired cane-bottomed chairs. He was a big fellow... hmmm... not very interesting. He used to drink and beat his wife.'

'So why have you put "a good father and a good husband" on his epitaph?'

'Because that's what you put on the graves of married people.'

'Who else has died since yesterday?'

'Mme Egrémimy Pulitien.'

'Who was she – Mme Egrémimy?...'

'Egrémimy, with a *y* at the end. Just a lady, always dressed in black. She wore cotton gloves...'

And my brother broke off, whistling through his teeth: the idea of cotton gloves rubbing against fingernails had set them on edge.

He was thirteen, and I was seven. With his black, close-cropped hair and his pale blue eyes he resembled a young Italian artist's model. He was extremely gentle, and completely uncontrollable.

'By the way,' he continued, 'be ready at ten o'clock to-morrow. There's a service.'

'What service?'

'A service for the repose of the soul of Lugustu Trutrumèque.'

'The father or the son?'

'The father.'

'At ten o'clock I can't, I'll be at school.'

'That's a shame; it means you won't see the service. Leave me alone now, I need to think of an epitaph for Mme Egrémimy Pulitien.'

Despite this warning, which rang out like an order, I followed my brother to the loft. On a trestle table he cut out and stuck together sheets of white cardboard, which he shaped into flat slabs, steles rounded at the top, or rectangular mausoleums surmounted by a cross. Then, in ornate capital letters, he painted epitaphs on them in China ink: long or short epitaphs that perpetuated, in pure 'marbler' style, the sorrows of the living and the virtues of some imaginary departed person.

'*Here rests Astoniphronque Bonscop, who passed away on 22nd June 1884, at the age of fifty-seven years. A good father and a good husband: earth's loss is heaven's gain. Passer-by, pray for him!*'

These few words stood out in black lines on a pretty tombstone shaped like a Romanesque portal, with *trompe-l'oeil* mouldings done in watercolour. A strut similar to the one that props up photograph-stands held it gracefully tilted backwards.

'The words are a bit dry,' said my brother. 'But a town crier… I'll make up for it with Madame Egrémimy.'

He condescended to read me a first draft.

' "*O model of Christian wives! You passed away at the age of eighteen, a mother four times over! The weeping and lamenting of your children could not hold you back! Now your business is foundering, your husband seeks oblivion in vain!…*" That's as far as I've got.'

'It's a nice start. Did she really have four children at the age of eighteen?'

'That's what I said.'

'And her business is foundling? What's that, a business that's foundling?'

my very eyes imaginary personages, transparent and yet visible, whom I could greet and ask for news of their family and friends, my brother invented dead people, treating them with every cordiality, and arraying them to the best of his abilities: one was surmounted by a cross with beams of light radiating out from it, another was laid to rest under a Gothic ogive arch, and a third was covered by nothing more than an epitaph singing the praises of his earthly life.

A day came when the rough floor of the loft was no longer good enough. My brother decided that he wanted to honour his white tombs with soft, fragrant earth, real grass, ivy and cypress trees... At the bottom of the garden, behind the grove of thuja trees, he found a place for his dear departed with their resounding names: there were so many of them that they overflowed the lawn, strewn with marigold heads and little wreaths of beads. The diligent gravedigger would scrutinise them with his artist's eye.

'That looks really good!'

After a week, my mother happened to pass by that way, and stopped, flabbergasted, staring with all her eyes – pince-nez, lorgnette, and glasses for distance – and uttered a cry of horror, violating all those burial places with a kick of her foot...

'That child's going to end up in the loony bin! It's madness, it's sadism, it's vampirism, it's sacrilege, it's... I really don't know what it is!...'

She gazed at the culprit across the abyss that separates a grown-up from a child. With angry pulls on her rake she swept up the gravestones, the wreaths and the broken columns. My brother endured without protest this public obloquy meted out to his labours and, staring at the denuded lawn and the hedge of thujas which cast its shade onto the freshly raked soil, he called me to witness, with a poet's melancholy:

'Don't you think a garden without tombs looks sad?'

'My Father's Daughter'

When I turned fourteen, fifteen years old – long arms, a straight back, a dumpy little chin, blue-green eyes that slanted when I smiled – my mother started to look at me, as they say, with an odd expression on her face. She would sometimes drop her book or her needle on her knees, and direct at me over the tops of her glasses a grey-blue stare of astonishment and almost suspicion.

'What have I done now, Maman?'

'Well… you resemble my father's daughter.'

Then she frowned and picked up her needle or book again. One day, she added, to this by now traditional reply, 'You know who my father's daughter is?'

'But it's you, of course!'

'No, Mademoiselle, it's not me.'

'Oh!… So you're not your father's daughter?'

She laughed, not in the least scandalised at a liberty of language that she herself encouraged.

'Good Lord, yes I am, just like the others, of course. There were… who knows how many? I myself only ever knew half of them. Irma, Eugène and Paul, and me, we all came from the same mother – we never really knew her. But as for you, you resemble my father's daughter, the daughter he brought home to us one day, newborn, without even bothering to tell us where she came from – just imagine! Oh, he was an old gorilla… You see how ugly he was, Little-Darling? Well, women all hung on him…'

She raised her thimble to the daguerreotype hanging on the wall, the daguerreotype that I now keep locked away in a drawer, and which contains, beneath its silvering, the head-and-shoulders portrait of a 'man of colour' – a quadroon, I believe, with a high white cravat, pale and contemptuous eyes, and a long nose over the thick Negro lips that were the reason for his nickname.

'Ugly, but well built,' my mother continued. 'And seductive, I can assure you, in spite of his purple fingernails. The only thing I don't like about him is that I inherited his horrid mouth.'

A big mouth, admittedly, but a kindly one, rosy red.

I protested, 'Oh, no! *You're* pretty.'

'I know what I'm talking about. At least I haven't passed on that mouth... My father's daughter arrived when I was eight. The Gorilla told me, "You can raise her. She's your sister." He always addressed us children formally. At the age of eight, I didn't think twice about it, since I didn't know anything about children. Fortunately, there was a nursemaid who came with my father's daughter. But while I was holding her in my arms, I had time to notice that her fingers didn't seem tapered enough. My father was so passionate about lovely hands... And there and then, with all the cruelty of children, I moulded those little fingers that were so soft they positively melted between mine... My father's daughter started life with ten little rounded abscesses, five on each hand, on the edges of those finely chiselled little fingernails. Yes... you can see how wicked your mother is... Such a beautiful newborn she was... She really screamed. The doctor said, "I just can't understand this inflammation on her fingers..." and I trembled. But I didn't own up. Children have such a strong tendency to lie... They generally grow out of it, later on... Are you starting to lie a bit less now you're growing up, Little-Darling?'

This was the first time that my mother had accused me of chronic lying. All the perverse or delicate dissembling that is part and parcel of adolescence suddenly evaporated when she turned on it her deep gaze – grey, divinatory and disabused... But already the hand she had lightly placed on my forehead had withdrawn, and her grey eyes, regaining their gentleness and sense of scruple, turned forgivingly away from mine.

'I really did take care of her afterwards, you know – my father's daughter… I learnt how to. She turned into a pretty girl, tall, blonder than you are – and you look like her, you look just like her… I think she got married very young… I'm not sure. That's all I know: my father took her away, later on, just as he'd first brought her, without condescending to tell us a thing. She just spent her first years with us – Eugène, Paul, Irma and me – and with Jean the big monkey, in the house where my father made chocolate. In those days, chocolate was made with cocoa, sugar and vanilla. At the top of the house, bricks of chocolate were laid out on the terrace while still soft, to dry. And every morning, there were slabs of chocolate marked by the imprints – flower shapes with five petals – of the cats' nightly peregrinations… I missed my father's daughter, Little-Darling: and just think…'

The rest of the conversation has gone missing from my memory. It cuts out just as brutally as if I had become deaf at just that moment. The reason was that I was indifferent to My-Father's-Daughter, and left my mother to summon up from oblivion the dead people she had loved, while I continued to hang dreamily on a perfume or an image that she had evoked: the odour of the chocolate in its soft bricks, and the hollow flowers that had bloomed under the paws of the wandering cat.

The Wedding

Henriette Buisson isn't going to get married. I know I can't count on her. She's promenading her round little belly in front of her, seven months gone, though this doesn't prevent her from scrubbing the kitchen tiles, or hanging out the washing on clothes-lines and on the spindle-tree hedge. In my part of the world, you don't get married if you've got a belly like that. Mme Pomié and Mme Léger have told my mother twenty times over, 'I can't understand why, when you've got a big girl like your daughter, you keep on a servant who's... a servant that someone's...'

But my mother roundly declared that she'd rather have 'people pointing fingers at her' than throw a mother and her baby out onto the streets.

So, Henriette Buisson isn't going to get married. But Adrienne Septmance, who occupies the post of chambermaid in our family, is pretty and lively, and for the past month she's been singing a great deal. She sings as she sews, and pins to her neck a bow where a border of interwoven lace and satin surrounds a pattern of lead imitating marcasite. She plants a pearl-edged comb in her black hair, and on her inflexible busk she straightens out the folds of her brightly dyed cotton blouse every time she passes in front of a mirror. I'm experienced enough not to be deceived by these symptoms. I'm thirteen and a half, and I recognise a chambermaid who's got herself a boyfriend. Will Adrienne Septmance get married? That is the question.

The Septmance household includes four daughters, three boys, and assorted cousins, all of them living together under one ancient, flowering thatch roof by the roadside.

What a lovely wedding I'm going to see! My mother will moan about it for a whole week, she'll go on about the 'bad company' I'm keeping, and my 'lack of manners'; she'll threaten to come with me whenever I go there, only to abandon the idea out of weariness and natural lack of sociability…

I keep spying on Adrienne Septmance. She sings, finishes her work as quickly as she can, rushes out into the street, and utters a shrill, artificial laugh.

Around her I catch a whiff of that common scent, available locally at Maumond's, the hairdresser's; it's a scent that you can apparently smell with your tonsils, and it makes you think of the sweet urine of horses drying on the roads…

'Adrienne, you smell of patchouli!' declares my mother, even though she never actually knew what patchouli was…

Finally, in the kitchen, I encounter a dark-haired young lad with a white straw hat, sitting propped against the wall and as silent as any boy who's come here for the right reason. I exult, and my mother looks grave.

'Who are we going to get once she's gone?' she asks my father during dinner.

But has my father even noticed that Adrienne Septmance has succeeded Marie Bardin?

'They've invited us to the wedding,' my mother adds. 'I won't be going, of course. Adrienne asked me if Little One could be a bridesmaid… It's really awkward.'

'Little One' is already on her feet and launches out on her pre-prepared tirade.

'Maman, I can go with Julie David and all the Follet girls. You know perfectly well you don't need to worry yourself if all the Follet girls are going, Mme Follet's cart will take us there and bring us back, and she's said that her daughters wouldn't be dancing any later than ten o'clock and…'

I blush and stumble to a halt, since my mother, instead of starting to moan, looks me up and down with an expression of extremely sardonic contempt.

'I was thirteen and a half once,' she says. 'You don't need to talk about it till you're blue in the face. Just say, "I *love* servants' weddings".'

* * *

My white dress with its purple sash, my hair hanging loose and making me feel hot, my golden-brown shoes – too short, too short – and my white stockings: they've all been ready since yesterday. Indeed, my hair has been plaited to give it a wave, and it's been pulling on my temples for forty-eight hours.

The weather is fine, scorchingly hot, typical weather for a country wedding; Mass didn't go on too long. The Follet son gave me his arm in the procession, but after the procession, what do you expect him to do with a thirteen-year-old partner?... Mme Follet is driving the cart that we fill to overflowing, uttering peals of laughter, with her four daughters all alike dressed in blue, and Julie David in shot mauve and pink alpaca. The carts dance along the road and now comes the moment I like best of all...

Wherever did I get it from, this intense passion for the feasts served up at country weddings? Which ancestor bequeathed to me, via such frugal parents, this almost religious devotion to sautéed rabbit, gigot with garlic, soft-boiled eggs with red wine, all served in the barnyard, the walls of which are draped with unbleached sheets with June roses, glowing red, pinned to them? I'm only thirteen, and the familiarity of the menu of these four-o'clock meals never, in my case, breeds contempt. Glass fruit bowls filled with sugar lumps line the table: as everyone knows, they're only here so that between one course and the next we can suck sugar dipped in wine – it unties our tongues and rekindles the appetite. Bouilloux and Labbé, those gargantuan freak shows, see who can stuff himself fastest, here at the

Septmances' just as they do wherever there's a wedding. Labbé drinks white wine from a pail used for milking cows, and Bouilloux watches as a whole leg of lamb is brought to him: he eats the lot, leaving nothing but the bare bone.

Singing and feasting and drinking: Adrienne's wedding is a very fine affair. Five meat courses, three desserts and a nougat-topped wedding cake, on which there trembles a rose made of plaster. Since four o'clock the wide-open barnyard door has framed the green pond sheltered by elm trees, and a stretch of sky in which the pink hues of evening are slowly rising. Adrienne Septmance, raven-haired and transformed in her cloud of tulle, languorously presses her head to her husband's shoulder and wipes his face on which the sweat gleams. A tall bony peasant bellows patriotic couplets: 'We must save Paris! We must save Paris!', and everyone looks fearfully at him, as his voice is loud and melancholy and he himself has come from a long way away. 'Just think! A man who lives in Dampierre-sous-Bouhy! At least thirty kilometres from here!' The swallows shriek, darting about on their hunting expeditions above the drinking cattle. The bride's mother, for some reason, is crying. Julie David has stained her dress; the four Follet girls are dressed in blue: in the gathering gloom they look as blue as phosphorus. The candles won't be lit until the dancing begins… A happiness for which I am still too young, the subtle happiness of a replete greedy-guts, keeps me sitting there feeling really mellow, stuffed with gravy, rabbit, chicken in a white wine sauce, and sweetened wine…

Rouillard's fiddle starts to scrape, giving all the Follet girls itchy feet – as well as Julie, and the bride, and the young farmers' wives with their goffered bonnets. 'Take your places for the quadrille!' Labbé and Bouilloux are no longer fit for anything: they're dragged outside with the trestle tables and the benches. The lingering dusk of June gives a heady intensity to the aroma of the pigsty and rabbit hutch nearby. I am empty of all desire, too full to dance, looking disdainful and superior like anyone who has eaten more than she should have. I really think that – as far as I am concerned – the carousing is over...

'Come for a walk with us,' says Julie David.

She drags me off to the farm's kitchen garden. The crushed sorrel, the sage and the green leeks fill the air with their incense as we walk through them, and my friend talks non-stop. Her hair, which had been kept in place by a huge quantity of double pins, is no longer as curly as a sheep's fleece, and her skin, white against her blond hair, is as smooth and glistening on her cheeks as a well-polished apple.

'The Caillon boy gave me a kiss... I heard everything the bridegroom has just been telling his bride... he said, "Just one more schottische and then to blazes with them"... Armandine Follet threw up in front of everyone...'

I feel hot. Her moist girlish arm sticks to mine. I pull away. I don't like the skin of other people... At the rear of the farmhouse there's one window open, all lit up; the mosquitoes and hawkmoths are dancing around a smoking Pigeon oil lamp.[32]

'That's the young couple's bedroom!' whispers Julie.

The young couple's bedroom... A huge wardrobe of black pear-wood dominates that low-ceilinged, white-walled room, crushing a straw-bottomed chair between itself and the bed. Two enormous bouquets of roses and camomile, bound up like bundles of twigs, are wilting on the mantelpiece, in vases of blue glass, and from them there wafts out into the garden the pervasive, strong, faded scent that hangs around in the air after a funeral... Under its curtains of Adrianople red, the tall, narrow bed, the bed stuffed with down and crammed with goose-down pillows, the bed that is to be the final scene of this wedding day all steaming with sweat, incense, the breath of cattle, the aroma of different sauces...

The wing of a geometer moth sputters in the flame of the lamp and almost extinguishes it. I lean on the low window sill and breathe in that human smell, with its sharp edge of dead flowers and paraffin, sullying the garden. Shortly, the young couple will be arriving here. I hadn't thought of that. They will dive into that deep mound of feathers. The massive shutters and the door will be closed behind them – no exit from this suffocating little tomb. They will embark on that obscure struggle about which my mother's bold and direct language and the life of animals have taught me both too much and too little... And then?... I'm afraid of that bedroom, afraid of that bed which I hadn't thought of. My friend laughs and chatters...

'Gosh, did you see that the Follet boy placed the rose I gave him in his buttonhole? Gosh, did you see that Nana Bouilloux has put her hair up? And she's only thirteen, you know!... When *I* get married, I won't hesitate to tell Maman... But where are you going? Where are you going?'

I am running, trampling underfoot the lettuces and the ridges of the asparagus bed.

'Hey, wait for me! Whatever's the matter?'

Julie doesn't catch up with me until I've reached the gate to the kitchen garden, under the red halo of dust bathing the lamps of the dance floor, near the barnyard filled with the blare of a trombone, laughter and stamping feet – that reassuring barnyard where her impatience is finally greeted by a reply she would never have expected, a reply that I bleat out, sobbing like a little girl lost:

'I want to go and find Maman...'

My Sister with the Long Hair

I was twelve years old, with the language and the manners of a clever if gruff boy, but my odd appearance wasn't that of a tomboy, since my body already had a feminine figure, and in particular I wore two long plaits that swished like whips around me. I used them as ropes to pass through the handle of the picnic basket, as brushes to dip into ink or paint, as straps to keep the dog under control, and as ribbons for the cat to play with. My mother groaned at the sight of me massacring these thongs of golden-brown hair which obliged me to get up half an hour earlier than my schoolmates each morning. On dark winter mornings, at seven o'clock, I would doze off to sleep again as I sat there, in front of the wood fire, while my mother brushed and combed my nodding head. My fixed aversion to long hair dates back to those mornings… Long hair kept getting entangled in the lower branches of the garden trees, and long hair snagged in the cross-beam from which hung the trapeze and the swing. We thought a farmyard chick must have been born lame, until we discovered that a long hair, covered with pimply skin, had got tightly wrapped round one of its feet and was preventing it from growing…

Ah, long hair! You are a barbarian adornment, a fleece where lurks the odour of a beast, that we cherish in secret for secret purposes, that we display when you are all twisted and plaited, but conceal when you are hanging loose – who bathes in your flood as it cascades down to the waist? If anyone intrudes on a woman doing her hair, she flees as if she were naked. Love and the boudoir see little more of you than does the passer-by. If left to hang free, you fill the bed with the toils of a mesh that a sensitive skin finds irritating, and with strands of grass in which the wandering hand gets entangled. And yet there is one moment, in the evening, when the pins fall and the face glimmers shyly between tangled waves – and there is another, similar instant, in the morning… And because of those two instants, everything I have just written against you, long hair, becomes quite insignificant.

* * *

With my hair done Alsatian style, two little ribbons dangling at the end of my two plaits and a parting down the middle of my head, looking really quite ugly with my exposed temples and my ears too far away from my nose, I would sometimes pop upstairs to visit my sister with the long hair. At midday she would already be reading, since lunch finished at eleven o'clock. In the mornings, while still in bed, she would again be reading. The noise of the door opening hardly made her lift her black Mongolian eyes, preoccupied as they were by the love story or the blood-and-thunder adventure which veiled her gaze. A burnt-out candle clearly showed that she had spent the night awake. The bedroom wallpaper, pearl-grey with cornflowers, bore the traces, near the bed, of the matches that my sister with the long hair had been striking on it all night long, with careless brutality. Her chaste nightdress, with its long sleeves and little turned-down collar, allowed only her striking head to emerge, attractively ugly, with high cheekbones, and the sarcastic mouth of a pretty Kalmuck. Her thick, restless eyebrows moved like two silky caterpillars, and her low forehead, the nape of her neck, and her ears – all of her white, slightly anaemic flesh – seemed foredoomed to be overrun by her all-encroaching hair.

Her hair was so abnormally long, strong and thick that I never saw it arousing – as it deserved to arouse – either admiration or jealousy. My mother talked of it as if it were some incurable illness. 'Good Lord, I'd better go and comb Juliette's hair!' she would sigh. On days when we didn't have to go to school,

I would see my mother plod wearily downstairs from the first floor: she threw down the assortment of combs and brushes, saying, 'I've had enough… My left leg hurts… I've just been combing Juliette's hair.'

Juliette's hair – black, with a hint of auburn here and there, and gently waved – covered her exactly from head to toe when it was let down. As my mother undid her daughter's plaits, a black curtain fell, completely hiding her back; her shoulders, her face and her skirt all disappeared in succession, and all that you could see before you was a strange conical tent made of dark silk with great parallel waves, parting briefly to reveal an Asiatic face, and rippled by two little hands that felt their way up and down the fabric of the tent.

This shelter was folded into four plaits – four cables as thick as a sturdy wrist, and glittering like water-snakes. Two of them sprang from the level of her temples, two others from above the nape of her neck, pulled to either side of a narrow parting of bluish skin. A sort of ridiculous diadem then crowned the young brow, and, lower down, another confection of plaits imposed its burden on the humiliated neck. The yellowing portraits of Juliette prove it: never did a young girl have a worse hairstyle.

'Poor little thing!' Mme Pomié would exclaim, clasping her hands together.

'Can't you at least put your hat on straight?' Mme Donnot asked Juliette as they came out of church after Mass. 'It's true that, with your hair… Ah, you have to admit that it must be difficult to live with hair like yours…'

So, on Thursday mornings, at around ten o'clock, I would quite often find my sister with the long hair still in bed, reading. She was always pale and absorbed, and she read with an air of fierce concentration, having let the cup of chocolate next to her grow cold. When I came in, she hardly turned her head; she similarly barely acknowledged the calls of 'Juliette, *do* get up!'

rising from the ground floor. She carried on reading, absently coiling one of her serpentine plaits around her wrist, and her gaze would sometimes casually fall on me: it was the gaze of obsessives, that gaze which has neither age nor sex, charged with an obscure mistrust and an unfathomable irony.

In this young girl's bedroom I savoured a distinguished sense of boredom that made me feel proud. The rosewood secretaire was stuffed to overflowing with inaccessible marvels: my sister with the long hair was a dab hand with the box of pastels; the box containing the compasses; and a certain piece of transparent white horn in a half-moon shape, engraved with centimetres and millimetres, the memory of which sometimes makes my palate water as if I had tasted a slice of lemon. The tracing paper for embroideries, all greasy, and as dark blue as the night sky; the punch used to pierce the 'wheels' in *broderie anglaise*; the tatting shuttles, the almond-white ivory shuttles and the bobbins of peacock-coloured silk, and the Chinese bird, painted on rice paper that my sister was copying in satin stitch on a velvet panel... And the invitations to the ball with their mother-of-pearl leaves, stuck to the superfluous fan of a young girl who never goes to the ball.

Once my fervent longings had been assuaged, I started to feel bored. And yet, if I looked through the window, I could gaze down into the Garden Opposite,[33] where our cat Zoë was tearing strips off some tomcat. And yet, in the adjoining garden (Mme Saint-Alban's), the rare clematis – the one that displayed slender mauve veins under the white pulpy flesh of its flower, like a sluggish trickle of blood under a delicate skin – opened into a dazzling cascade of six-pointed stars...

And yet, to the left, at the corner of the narrow rue des Soeurs, there was Tatave, the lunatic who everyone said was harmless, kicking up a horrible din, though not a single feature of his face moved... All the same, I was bored.

'What are you reading, Juliette?... Hey, Juliette, what are you reading?... Juliette!...'

I had to wait ages and ages for the reply, as if mile upon mile of space and silence lay between us.

'*Fromont the Younger and Risler the Elder.*'

Or:

'*The Charterhouse of Parma.*'

The Charterhouse of Parma, The Vicomte de Bragelonne, Monsieur de Camors, The Vicar of Wakefield, A Chronicle of Charles IX, The Earth, Lorenzaccio, The Monsters of Paris, Grande Maguet, Les Misérables...[34] Poetry too, though less often. Serialised stories from *Le Temps*, cut out and sewn together; the collection of the *Revue des Deux Mondes*, that of the *Revue Bleue*, that of the *Journal des Dames et des Demoiselles*, Voltaire and Ponson du Terrail...[35] Novels lay stuffed into cushions, overflowed from the work-basket, or were left forgotten in the garden where they melted away in the rain. My sister with the long hair had stopped speaking, hardly ate anything, seemed surprised when she encountered us in the house, and jumped in alarm when anyone rang the doorbell.

My mother was vexed, and stayed awake at night to extinguish Juliette's lamp and confiscate her candles: my sister with the long hair caught a cold and requested a night light to be placed in her room so she could make a hot infusion for herself: then she read by the flame of the night light. After the night light there were the boxes of matches and the moonlight. After the moonlight... After the moonlight, my sister with the long hair, worn out by novel-induced insomnia, went down with a fever, and the fever would yield neither to compresses nor to purgative water.

'A case of typhoid,' said Dr Pomié one morning.

'Typhoid? Come now, Doctor... Why? That can't be your final word?'

My mother was astonished, vaguely scandalised, but not yet worried. I remember her standing on the doorstep, cheerfully waving Dr Pomié's prescription as if it were a handkerchief.

'Goodbye, Doctor!… See you soon!… Yes, yes, that's right, do call round again tomorrow!'

She filled the entire threshold with her buxom agility, and she scolded the dog who was refusing to come inside. With the prescription in her fingers, the corners of her mouth turned downwards in a dubious pout, she went back to my sister, whom we had left sleeping and murmuring in her fever. Juliette had now woken up; her Mongol eyes, and her four plaits glistened darkly against the white bed.

'You can stay in bed for today, my darling,' said my mother. 'Dr Pomié has ordered you to. Now… would you like a nice cool glass of lemonade? Shall I remake your bed a bit?'

My sister with the long hair didn't reply straight away. And yet her slanting eyes looked us up and down alertly, with a new smile in them – a smile desirous to please. After a brief silence:

'Is that you, Catulle?' she asked in a light voice.

My mother started, and then took a step forward.

'Catulle? Catulle who?'

'Catulle Mendès,[36] of course,' the light voice replied. 'Is that you? I've come, you see. I've put your blond hair in the oval locket. Octave Feuillet[37] came this morning, but what a difference!… Judging simply from his photo, I'd thought… I can't stand sideburns. And in any case, I only like fair-haired men. Did I tell you I'd put a bit of red pastel on your photo, just where the mouth is? It's because of your poems… It must be that little red spot that's been giving me such a headache, ever since… No, we won't meet anyone… In any case, I don't know anyone that lives in this part of the world. It's because of that little red spot… and the kiss… Catulle… I don't know anyone here. In the presence of all those here assembled I swear that you alone, Catulle, are the one...'

My sister stopped talking and moaned in a shrill, intolerant tone, turning to the wall and continuing to moan much more softly, as if from a long way away. One of her plaits lay across her face: a shining plait, plump and bursting with life. My mother, motionless, had leant forward to hear and see more clearly, with a kind of horror, how this quite unrecognisable girl, in her delirium, was summoning to her bedside nobody but complete strangers. Then she looked round, noticed I was there, and hastily ordered me: 'Downstairs! Quickly...'

And, as if overwhelmed by shame, she hid her face in her two hands.

Motherhood

As soon as she was married, my sister with the long hair succumbed to the suggestions of her husband and her in-laws, and stopped seeing us, while the formidable machinery of notaries and lawyers was set in motion. I was eleven or twelve, and I didn't understand anything of the phrases ('improvident guardianship', 'inexcusable extravagance' and the like) that were aimed at my father.[38] There ensued a complete breaking-off of relations between the young couple and my parents. For my brothers and myself, this didn't lead to any great change. Whether my half-sister – that graceful, shapely girl with her Kalmuck face, overloaded with hair, and buried under her plaits as if they were chains – locked herself away in her room all day or went off into exile in a house nearby with a husband, made no great difference to us and didn't put us out in the slightest. In any case, my brothers lived far away, and they picked up only the muted aftershocks of an upheaval that kept our whole village preoccupied. A family tragedy in a big city evolves discreetly, and its heroes can clash without creating much of a stir. But a village lives all year round in a state of uneventful peace and quiet, and has to satisfy its hunger with meagre titbits of gossip about poaching or flirtations – such a village is pitiless, and nobody kindly and discreetly averts their gaze as a woman goes by who has been robbed of her child in less than a day because of difficulties over money.

We were the topic of every conversation. People queued up at Léonore's, the butcher's, every morning to meet my mother and oblige her to surrender a piece of herself. Creatures who, the day before, had not shown the least sign of bloodthirsty curiosity now shared some of her precious tears, and the complaints of maternal indignation torn from her bosom. She would return home exhausted, panting like a beast pursued.

She would start to feel a little braver once she was at home, between my father and me, where she would cut up the bread for the chickens, baste the roast on its spit, and nail together, with all the strength of the small hands at the end of her sturdy arms, a box for the cat who was about to give birth to her kittens. She would wash my hair with egg yolk and rum. She deployed a sort of cruel art in suppressing her grief, and sometimes I heard her sing. But in the evenings she would climb upstairs to close with her own hands the shutters on the first floor, so that she could first peer at the garden and the house where my sister lived, over the dividing wall that separated them from the Garden Opposite. She could see strawberry beds, rows of apple trees and clumps of phlox, and three steps leading to a terrace decorated with orange trees in tubs and wicker chairs. One evening – I was standing behind her – I recognised on one of the chairs a purple and gold shawl, which dated from the last convalescence of my sister with the long hair. I exclaimed, 'Oh, look, is that Juliette's shawl?', and received no reply. A strange, convulsive sound, like that of stifled laughter, faded away down the corridor with my mother's footsteps, once she had closed all the shutters.

Months went by and nothing changed. The ungrateful daughter remained beneath her roof, and walked stiffly past our front door, but if she happened to bump into my mother, she would run away like a little girl afraid of getting a smack. When I met her, I felt no emotion, and was simply rather surprised at this strange woman wearing unfamiliar hats and new dresses.

One day, the rumour spread that she was going to have a child. But I hardly thought about her any more, and I paid no attention to the fact that, at just that moment, my mother suffered from attacks of intense nervous faintness, nausea and palpitations. I merely remember that the sight of my sister looking misshapen and heavy of gait filled me with confusion and disgust...

More weeks went by... My mother, still lively and active, deployed her energies in a somewhat incoherent way. One day she sugared the strawberry tart with salt, and instead of getting upset about it she greeted my father's rebukes with a stony, ironic face that really distressed me.

One summer evening, as all three of us were finishing dinner, a neighbour came in bareheaded. She wished us good evening in rather an affected tone of voice, whispered a few mysterious words into my mother's ear, and immediately left. My mother sighed, 'Oh my God!...' and stayed standing there, her hands resting on the table.

'What's the matter?' my father asked.

She made an effort and pulled her gaze away from absorbed contemplation of the lamp flame and replied:

'It's started... over there...'

I vaguely understood, and I was quicker than usual to run up to my bedroom, one of the three overlooking the Garden Opposite. Having extinguished my lamp, I opened my window to spy on the mysterious house at the end of the garden that was filled with purplish moonlight. All the shutters were closed. I listened, pressing my beating heart against the window ledge. The village imposed its usual nocturnal silence on the scene, and all I could hear was the barking of a dog and the claws of a cat lacerating the trunk of a tree. Then a shadowy figure in a white dressing gown – my mother – crossed the street, and entered the Garden Opposite. I saw her looking up, measuring with her eyes the dividing wall as if she were planning to climb over it. Then she walked up and down the short garden path in between, and mechanically broke off a short branch of fragrant laurel which she crushed in her fingers. In the chill light of the full moon, I could catch all her movements. Motionless, her face turned heavenwards, she listened, waiting. A prolonged, hovering cry, muffled by the distance and the closed shutters, reached her at the same time it reached me, and she vehemently clasped her hands to her breast. A second cry, held on the same note like the start of a melody, floated through the air, and then a third... Then I saw my mother enfolding her own belly in a tight embrace, and spin round, pawing the ground with her feet; and she started to help, mimicking – in her low groans, the swayings of her tormented body, and the hugging of her useless arms, and with all the maternal pain and strength she possessed – the pain and strength of that ungrateful girl who was giving birth so far away from her.

'Paris Fashions'

'Twenty sous for the front rows, ten sous for the second, five sous for children and standing room.' These used to be the prices of our artistic entertainments, whenever a troupe of strolling players stopped for an evening in my home village. The town crier, entrusted with the task of alerting the thirteen hundred souls in the canton's main town, announced the event at around ten o'clock in the morning with a roll of his drum. Wherever he went, the town blazed with excitement. Children like me jumped up and down on the spot, uttering shrill cries. Young girls, their hair bristling with curlers, stood for a moment rooted to the spot, dumbfounded with happiness, and then dashed off as if trying to escape a hailstorm. And my mother complained, not without a certain bad faith, 'Good heavens! Little-Darling, you're not going to drag me to see *A Woman's Torment* are you? It's so boring! The woman in torment will be me...' All the same, she prepared the goffering and the pleating irons so that she herself could frill out her prettiest 'shirt-front' of fine linen...

Smoky lamps with tin reflectors, benches harder than those at school, canvas scenery with flaking paint, actors as glum as captive animals – with what melancholy did you ennoble my evening pleasure... For the dramas filled me with a glacial horror, and when I was young I was never really able to enjoy those tattered vaudeville pieces, or to echo the laughter aroused by down-at-heel comedians.

What chance was it that brought to us one day, fully equipped with scenery and costumes, a real troupe of itinerant players, all of them in nice clean clothes, not looking too undernourished, and all under the thumb of a sort of squire wearing boots and a dicky of white piqué? We didn't hesitate – my father, my mother and I – before paying three francs each to watch *The Tower of Nesle*.[39] But the new price alarmed our rather tight-fisted village, and the very next day, the troupe left us to pitch its tents at X***, a small neighbouring town, an aristocratic and coquettish kind of place, huddled at the foot of its castle and bowing in obeisance to its titled owners. *The Tower of Nesle* packed them in, and after the play the lady of the manor publicly congratulated M. Marcel d'Avricourt, the star of the show, a tall, likeable young man, who handled his sword like a real professional and whose luxuriant eyelashes veiled lovely antelope eyes. This was quite enough to persuade everyone to swelter their way through *Denise*,[40] the following evening. The day after that, a Sunday, M. d'Avricourt attended the eleven o'clock Mass in a morning coat, offered the holy water to two blushing young girls, and strode off without paying the least attention to their excitement – a discretion which the whole town of X*** was still praising a few hours later, at the matinée performance of *Hernani*,[41] where some potential spectators had to be turned away.

The wife of the young notary of X*** was no wallflower. She permitted herself the sudden, girlishly impulsive decisions of a woman who copied the dresses worn by 'those ladies up in the castle', sang as she played the piano, and wore her hair in a fringe. The following day, at dawn, she went off to order a *vol-au-vent* at the Hôtel de la Poste, where M. d'Avricourt was staying, and listened to the gossip of the manageress.

'For eight people, Madame? Saturday at seven o'clock, without fail! I'll just pour out Monsieur d'Avricourt's warm milk and then I'll make a note of your order… Yes, Madame, he is staying here… Ah! Madame, you'd never guess he was an actor! A voice like a young girl… And as soon as he has returned from his walk, after lunch, he goes up to his room and takes up his work.'

'His work?'

'He embroiders, Madame! He's so talented! He's just finishing a piano cover in satin stitch – it's good enough to be exhibited! My daughter has copied the design…'

The young notary's wife sought out M. d'Avricourt that very same day. She found him dreaming away under the lime trees, went up to him, and enquired after a certain piano cover whose design and execution... M. d'Avricourt blushed, modestly shaded his gazelle eyes with one hand, uttered two or three strange little shrieks and muttered a few embarrassed words.

'Childish pastimes!... Pastimes which Parisian fashions only encourage...'

He waved his hand with graceful affectation, as if to shoo away a fly, and brought his sentence to an end. To which the notary's wife replied with an invitation to take tea.

'Oh, a friendly little tea party where everyone can bring their work...'

During the week, *M. Poirier's Son-in-Law* was applauded to the skies, together with *Hernani*, *The Hunchback* and *Two Timid Fellows*, all greeted with the greatest enthusiasm by a public which never wearied of the fare.[42] M. d'Avricourt was received in the homes of the box-office lady, and the wives of the chemist and the tax collector: he dominated the proceedings with the colour of his cravats, and his way of walking, greeting people and uttering, in between the crystal shards of his laughter, high-pitched little giggles – not to mention the way he placed one hand on his hip as if on a sword-hilt, and the way he embroidered. The squire in boots, lord and master of the theatrical troupe, enjoyed many a delightful hour, sent off money orders to the *Crédit Lyonnais*, and spent the afternoons at the Café de la Perle, in the company of the noble father, the big-nosed comedian, and the somewhat snub-nosed soubrette.

It was at just this moment that the lord of the manor, who'd been away for a fortnight, decided to return from Paris and seek the advice of the esteemed notary of X***. He found the notary's wife serving tea. Next to her, the senior clerk, a bony and ambitious giant of a man, was counting his stitches on the tightly stretched aida fabric of a tambour. The chemist's son, a little gadabout with the face of a coachman, was interweaving the initials of a monogram on a place mat, while stout Glaume, an eligible widower, was filling the chequered pattern on a slipper with squares of wool, alternating magenta with old gold. Even doddery old M. Demange was there, trying his hand on a piece of coarse canvas... M. d'Avricourt was standing erect reciting poetry, while a bevy of idle women heaved sighs of religious adoration all around him: his oriental gaze did not deign to lower itself to them.

I never found out exactly what sharp words, or even sterner silence, the lord of the manor used to castigate the 'latest Paris fashion' and illuminate the strangely darkened minds of those fine people who sat staring at him, their needles poised.

But I have heard it said, many a time, that the next morning the troupe struck camp and that at the Hôtel de la Poste nothing was left of Lagardère, Hernani, or the impertinent son-in-law of M. Poirier – nothing but a skein of silk and a thimble that had been left behind.

Young Bouilloux

She was so pretty, young Bouilloux, that we actually took notice of her. It doesn't often happen that little girls recognise beauty in one of their number, and pay homage to it. But the undeniable beauty of young Bouilloux disarmed us. Whenever my mother met her in the street, she would stop her and bend over her, the same way she did for her saffron yellow rose, her purple-flowering cactus, or her Azure Blue butterfly that lay sleeping and trustful on the rugged bark of the tree. She touched little Bouilloux's curly hair, as golden as a half-ripe chestnut, and her transparent, rosy-pink cheek; she gazed at the enormous eyelashes fluttering over the pool of her huge dark eyes, the teeth that gleamed between lips of unrivalled loveliness, and then let the child go, following her with her eyes, sighing:

'She's a marvel!…'

Several years went by, adding yet more graces to young Bouilloux. There were certain dates that our admiration for her commemorated: a prize-giving when young Bouilloux, shyly reciting an unintelligible fable in an indistinct mumble, was as resplendent beneath her tears as a peach in a shower of rain… Young Bouilloux's first communion caused a scandal: she went off for a quick half-pint after vespers, with her father, the pit sawyer, at the Café de Commerce, and that evening was seen at the public ball, where she danced, already cutting a feminine, coquettish figure as she swayed around on her white shoes.

With an air of pride – something to which she had already accustomed us – she later told us, at school, that she was going to start an apprenticeship.

'Oh?… Who with?'

'Madame Adolphe.'

'Ah!… Are you going to start earning straight away?'

'No, I'm only thirteen, I'll start earning next year.'

She left us without expressing much emotion, and we coldly let her go. Her beauty had already set her apart, and she had no friends at school, where she never learnt very much. Her days off school – Sunday and Thursday – might have brought her closer to us, but instead these days belonged to a rather 'disreputable' family, with eighteen-year-old girl cousins who lounged boldly on the doorstep, and brothers who were apprentice wheelwrights: at the age of fourteen they already 'wore ties' and smoked cigarettes, with their sisters hanging on their arms as they sauntered from the fairground shooting-gallery to the lively little bar that the widow Pimelle kept so well stocked.

I saw young Bouilloux the very next morning, as she was walking up the street towards the seamstress' workshop, and I was heading down to school. Filled with stupor and jealous admiration I stood rooted to the spot, on the rue des Soeurs side, staring after Nana Bouilloux as she strode away. She had exchanged her black smock and girlish short dress for a long skirt and a pleated blouse of pink sateen. An apron of elegant black mohair hung in front of her skirt, and her bouncy curls, tamed and twisted into a figure-of-eight, closely framed the lovely, unfamiliar shape of her round and imperious face: the only thing that was still childlike in her expression was her freshness and the as-yet-inexperienced boldness of a loose-living young village woman.

The older classes were buzzing with excitement that morning.

'I've seen Nana Bouilloux! She's in a long dress, my dear, she's wearing a long dress! With her hair in a bun! And a pair of scissors hanging from her belt!'

I rushed home at midday to announce, breathlessly, 'Maman! I've seen Nana Bouilloux! She was walking past our front door! She's in a long dress, Maman, she's wearing a long dress! And with her hair in a bun! And high heels, and a pair of...'

'Eat up, Little-Darling, eat up, your cutlet will get cold.'

'And an apron, Maman, oh! such a lovely little apron in mohair, just like silk!... Couldn't I...?'

'No, Little-Darling, you couldn't.'

'But after all, Nana Bouilloux can...'

'Yes, she can, and indeed she should, wear her hair in a bun, a short apron and a long skirt at the age of thirteen – it's the uniform of all girls like Bouilloux the world over, when they reach the age of thirteen – unfortunately.'

'But...'

'Oh yes, you'd like a complete uniform like young Bouilloux's. It's made up of all the bits and pieces you've just seen, plus: a letter well hidden in the apron pocket, a boyfriend who smells of wine and cheap cigars; two boyfriends, three boyfriends... and a little later... floods of tears... a sickly baby that's been hidden away crushed beneath the busk of a corset for months on end... *That*, Little-Darling, is the full uniform of girls like Bouilloux. Fancy wearing it?'

'Of course not, Maman... I just wanted to see if wearing my hair in a bun...'

My mother shook her head with grave malice.

'Oh no you don't! You can't have your hair in a bun without the apron, or the apron without the letter, the letter without the high-heeled shoes, or the shoes without... all the rest! The choice is yours!'

My yearnings soon faded away. The radiant young Bouilloux was soon nothing more than a daily passer-by, and I barely spared her a glance. In winter and summer she went bareheaded, and every week wore a different brightly coloured blouse. When it was bitterly cold, she wrapped a rather useless little shawl tightly round her slender shoulders. Erect and brightly radiant as a thorny rose, her eyelashes lowered onto her cheek or revealing her dark moist eyes, she deserved, a little more each day, to reign over great throngs, and to attract the gaze of all in her jewel-laden finery. Her chestnut-brown hair, its curly crinkles tamed, still revealed its little waves that caught the light in a haze of gold on the nape of her neck and round her ears. She always seemed vaguely offended, with her short velvety nostrils that made you think of a doe.

She turned fifteen and then sixteen – as did I. Apart from the fact that she laughed a great deal on Sundays, as she hung on the arms of her girl cousins and her brothers, to show off her teeth, Nana Bouilloux kept herself pretty well.

'I say, for a young Bouilloux girl, there's no faulting her!' was the general verdict.

She turned seventeen, then eighteen, with a complexion like a fruit that has been well sheltered from the wind, eyes that made people lower their gaze, and a way of walking that she'd picked up heaven knows where. She started to frequent the dance floors of fairgrounds and fêtes, where she danced like a madwoman; she would go out walking very late at night, strolling down highways and byways, a man's arm round her waist. She always had a sharp tongue, but she laughed a lot, and drove those who would have been happy just to love her to make somewhat bolder demands.

Once, on the evening of St John's Day,[43] she was dancing on the dance floor set up on the Place du Grand-Jeu, under the dim light of smelly paraffin lamps. Hobnailed boots kicked up the dust in the square, between the planks of the dance floor. As they danced, all the boys kept their hats on, as is only right and proper. Blonde girls started to turn a wine-dark colour in their tight, sticky bodices, while dark-haired girls from the fields, burnt by the sun, looked positively black. But, amid a band of disdainful work girls, Nana Bouilloux, in a summer dress decorated with little flowers, was drinking lemonade mixed with red wine when the Parisian lads arrived at the ball.

They were two Parisians of the kind you see in the country-side during the summer, friends of a nearby lord of the manor, and pretty bored; Parisians in tussore silk and white serge who were here just to have a quick laugh at the St John's Day festivities as celebrated in a village... The laughter died in their throats when they saw Nana Bouilloux and sat down at the bar to get a closer look. They exchanged a few hushed remarks which she pretended not to hear. The pride she took in her beauty prevented her from turning to look at them, or from laughing hysterically like the girls she was with. She heard them saying, 'A swan among geese... A real Greuze!⁴⁴... Criminal to let such a marvellous creature bury herself away out here...' When the Parisian in white serge invited young Bouilloux to waltz, she rose to her feet without showing the least surprise and danced in silence, with a serious expression; her eyelashes, lovelier than a glance, occasionally grazed the bristles of a fair moustache.

After the waltz, the Parisians left, and Nana Bouilloux sat at the bar, fanning herself. The Leriche boy came looking for her, and Houette, and even Honce, the chemist, and even Possy, the cabinet-maker, already turning grey but an excellent dancer. To all of them she replied, 'Many thanks, but I'm tired,' and she left the dance at half-past ten.

And after that, nothing more happened to young Bouilloux. The Parisians never returned, and nor did any other Parisian visitors. Houette, Honce, the Leriche boy, the commercial travellers with golden watch-chains dangling across their bellies, the soldiers on leave and the bailiff's clerks climbed up our steep street in vain, at the hours when she strode down it, an elegantly coiffured seamstress who passed by with a straight back and a mere nod. They waited for her at dances, where she drank lemonade with an air of distinction and replied to all requests, 'Many thanks, but I'm not dancing, I'm too tired'. Their feelings were hurt, and after a few days, they started to say, with a snigger, 'She's tired all right – she's got the kind of tiredness that lasts thirty-six weeks!' and they kept a sharp eye on her stomach... But nothing happened to young Bouilloux, neither that nor anything else. She was waiting, that was all. She was waiting, imbued by a proud faith, fully aware of what she was owed by the random destiny that had forearmed her so well. She was waiting for... that Parisian in white serge? No. The stranger, the ravisher. Her proud wait made her pure and silent, and she turned down, with a little smile of surprise, Honce, who wished to elevate her to the rank of a legitimate chemist's wife, and the bailiff's senior clerk. Without ever abasing herself again, and retrieving in one go all the things she had thrown away on her doters – laughter, glances, the glowing bloom on her cheek, her small, red, childlike lips, and a bosom with barely a blue shadow of cleavage – she awaited her reign, and her unknown prince.

When, a while ago, I passed through the area where I had been born, I did not find any shadow of the woman who so lovingly refused my request for what she called the 'uniform of young girls like Bouilloux'. But as the car which was carrying me climbed slowly – not slowly enough, never slowly enough – up a street where I no longer have any reason to stop off, a passing woman stepped aside to avoid the wheel. A slim, well-coiffured woman, her hair in the tight fashion of bygone days, and a seamstress' scissors hanging from a steel 'chatelaine' on her black apron. Big vindictive eyes, a tight mouth that probably stayed shut for long periods, the yellowed temple and cheeks of women who work by lamplight; a woman aged between forty-five and... No, no; a woman of thirty-eight, a woman my age, my age exactly, there could be no doubt about it... As soon as the car had made way for her, 'young Bouilloux' walked down the street, erect and indifferent, as soon as a bitter, anxious glance had told her that the car was going its way, and did not bring her long-awaited ravisher.

Toutouque

Broad and squat like a four-month-old piglet, with a smooth yellow coat, and a big black mask, she looked more like a little mastiff than a bulldog. Ignorant people had trimmed her shell-like ears into points and cropped her tail close to her rear. But never did any female in the world – whether dog or human being – receive, as her meed of beauty, eyes comparable to those of Toutouque. When my elder brother, who'd signed up for voluntary military service in the next big town, saved her from an idiotic regulation that condemned any dogs found in barracks to death, and brought her back to our house, she gazed upon us with her eyes the colour of old Madeira, barely troubled, penetrating, and gleaming with a moistness similar to that of human tears: we were all won over, and made ample room for Toutouque in front of the wood fire. We all appreciated – and I in particular did, being a young girl – her nanny-like cordiality and her even temper. She didn't bark very much, in her thick, muffled mastiff's voice, but had another way of communicating, expressing her opinion with a black-lipped, white-toothed smile, and lowering her coal-black eyelids with a conniving air over her mulatto eyes.

She learnt our names, a hundred new words, and the names of the female cats, just as quickly as a bright child would have done. She adopted us all in her heart, followed my mother to the butcher's, and walked part of the way to school with me every day. But she belonged exclusively to that elder brother who had saved her from the rope or the revolver shot. She loved him so much that she seemed abashed in his presence. For him she behaved in utterly silly ways, bowing her head, all too happy to seek out the torments that he imposed on her, even greeting them as rewards. She lay on her back, offering her belly, studded with little purple teats: which my brother's fingers would run up and down, playing, as if on a piano, the melody from Boccherini's Minuet, and pinching each of them in turn. The ritual decreed that, at every pinch, Toutouque should utter – as she unfailingly did – a short yelp, at which my brother sternly exclaimed, 'Toutouque! You're singing out of tune! Start again!' There was no cruelty in this: his grazing fingers simply tickled Toutouque and drew from her a series of varied musical cries. Once the game was over, she continued to lie there, begging for more.

My father repaid her devotion in kind, and composed for her those songs that involuntarily spring to our lips in moments of childish wildness and abandon – those strange offspring of rhythm and repetition, words that blossom into being in the innocence of empty heads. One refrain praised Toutouque for being:

> *Yellow, yellow, yellow,*
> *Excessively yellow,*
> *As yellow as yellow can be…*

Another refrain celebrated her massive girth, and hailed her three times over as a 'nice old cylinder', to the catchy beat of a military march. Then Toutouque would roar with laughter – that is, she would reveal the teeth between her puckering lips, flatten the clipped remains of her ears and, for lack of a tail, waggle her great posterior. Whether she was asleep in the garden, or employed on serious business in the kitchen, the song of the 'cylinder', sung by my brother, always brought Toutouque to her feet, captivated by the familiar harmony.

One day, after dinner, as Toutouque lay roasting herself on the scorching marble of the hearth, my brother sat down at the piano and inserted the song of the 'cylinder', without words, into the overture his fingers were strumming. The first notes droned past the drowsy ears of the sleeping beast like so many buzzing flies. Her pale fawn coat, smooth as a Jersey cow's, twitched here and there, and her ear... The vigorous da capo (for piano solo) half-opened her eyes, full of human puzzlement, and Toutouque, that musical old thing, got up and asked me, quite clearly, 'Haven't I heard that somewhere before?...' Then she turned to her ingenious tormentor who was still hammering out her favourite tune, accepted this new, magical homage from him, and went over to sit right next to the piano, so as to listen better, with the understanding and yet mystified expression of a child following a conversation between adults.

Her gentleness deprived all teasing of its aggression. We entrusted her with newborn kittens to be licked into shape, and the puppies of bitches from other houses. She would kiss the hands of toddlers, and allow chicks to peck her, and I despised her a little for her docility, so like that of a well-fed housewife, until one day when, in the fullness of time, Toutouque became enamoured of a hunting dog, the setter who belonged to the proprietor of a nearby café. He was a big setter, endowed, as are all setters, with a Second Empire charm; a blond mahogany in colour, long-haired, his eyes flecked with gold; his face showed no real breeding, but he was not without distinction. His mate resembled him like a sister; but she was highly strung and prone to fits of the vapours, started yelping as soon as anyone slammed a door shut, and whimpered at the sound of the angelus. For reasons of euphony alone, their master had named them Black and Bianca.

This brief idyll allowed me to get to know Toutouque better. Walking past the café with her one day, I saw the russet-coloured Bianca lying on the doorstep, her paws crossed, her ringlets hanging uncurled down her cheeks. The two bitch dogs exchanged but a single glance and Bianca uttered a shrill cry as if someone had trodden on her paw, before dashing for cover in the depths of the bar. Toutouque had not moved an inch from my side, and the expressive glint in her eye, that of a tipsy, sentimental old girl, seemed to say, 'What's wrong with her?'

'Leave her,' I replied, 'you know she's half crazy.'

Nobody at home bothered about Toutouque's personal affairs. She was free to come and go, to push the swing door with her nose, to say hello to the butcher's wife, or to join my father as he sat playing écarté; we were never afraid that Toutouque might get lost, or that she might indulge in mischief. So, when the café proprietor came to inform us – holding Toutouque responsible – that his bitch dog Bianca had got her ear torn, we all burst out into rude laughter, pointing to our Toutouque wallowing there blissfully, as an imperious little kitten carded her coat...

The next morning, I had perched myself like a stylite on the capital of one of the pillars between which the garden fence ran, and I was there, preaching to invisible crowds when I heard a mêlée of canine howls rushing up, dominated by the shrill, desperate yelping of Bianca. She came into view, tousled and haggard, darted across the corner of the rue de la Roche, and sped down the rue des Vignes. Hard on her heels there rolled, travelling at an unimaginable speed, a sort of yellow monster, its hair standing on end, its paws initially tucked under its belly and then flung out on every side, like frogs' legs, as it careered madly along – a yellow beast, with a black mask, garnished with teeth, eyes popping out of its head, and a purple tongue flecked with saliva... The whole caboodle swept by like a whirlwind and vanished. While I hurriedly climbed down from my capital, I made out in the distance the collision, and then the tempestuous snarling, of a very brief altercation, and then the voice of the red bitch dog, sounding wounded... I dashed across the garden, and reached the gate to the street, where I halted, stupefied: there was Toutouque, the monster I had just glimpsed, yellow and ferocious, lying on the doorstep...

'Toutouque!'

She sketched her nanny-like smile, but she was panting, and the whites of her eyes, streaked with threads of blood, seemed to be bleeding...

'Toutouque! Have you really...?'

She got up, squirmed with embarrassment and tried to change the subject, but her black lips, and the tongue that tried to lick my fingertips, was still covered by the golden-red hairs that she had torn out of Bianca...

'Oh, Toutouque!... Toutouque...'

I couldn't think of anything else to say, and didn't know how to express my dismay, my alarm and my amazement that some malevolent force, the very name of which was unknown to me at the age of ten, could change the gentlest of creatures into a savage brute.

The Spahi's Cloak

The spahi's cloak, the black burnous with gold lamé stripes, the chechia,[45] the 'jewels' composed of three oval miniatures – a locket and two earrings – surrounded by a garland of tiny precious stones, the piece of 'real Spanish hide' that was indelibly perfumed... these were all treasures which I once viewed with reverence. And in so doing, I was merely imitating my mother.

'They're not toys,' she would declare gravely, but her tone of voice did indeed make me think of toys, albeit toys for grown-ups...

She would sometimes amuse herself by draping the burnous over me; black, with stripes of gold lamé, it was of no great weight. On my head she would place the tasselled hood, whereupon she congratulated herself for having given birth to me.

'You can keep it and wear it when you're married and it's time to come home after a ball,' she would say. 'There's nothing that looks more becoming, and at any rate it's the kind of item of clothing that's never out of fashion. Your father brought it back from his stint in Africa, with the spahi's cloak.'

The spahi's cloak was red, made of fine cloth; it slept folded away in an old, worn sheet, and my mother had slipped in between its folds a cigar cut into four pieces and a seasoned meerschaum pipe, 'to protect against moths'. Did the moths get used to it, or did the dottle in the pipe lose its insecticidal virtue as it grew old? During one of those household catastrophes known as 'spring cleanings', which, like surging rivers smashing through their ice, break up the seals of linen, paper and string in the cupboards, my mother, as she shook out the spahi's cloak, uttered a great cry of lament.

'It's been eaten!'

The family came rushing up as if to see a cannibal feast, and pored over the cloak where the daylight was shining in through a hundred holes, as round as if the fine cloth had been riddled by machine-gun fire.

'Eaten!' my mother repeated. 'And there's my red fox fur, right next to it, untouched.'

'Eaten!' said my father, calmly. 'Well, there we are, it's been eaten.'

My mother drew herself up before him like some Fury of housekeeping.

'Well, you don't seem particularly bothered, I must say!'

'Not particularly, no,' said my father. 'I'm used to it already.'

'Oh, *men*…!'

'I know. Anyway, what had you been keeping this cloak for?'

She immediately lost her self-assured air and looked as perplexed as a cat when you offer it milk in a bottle whose neck is too narrow.

'What…? I was keeping it! It's been in the same sheet for fifteen years. Twice a year I'd unfold it, give it a good shake and fold it back up again…'

'Well you won't have to worry about doing that any more. Instead, you can concentrate on the green tartan plaid, since it's a well-known fact that your family has the right to use the red and white one, but nobody is allowed to touch the green, blue and yellow one.'

'The green plaid is the one I put over Little One's legs when she's poorly.'

'That's not true.'

'What? Now what do you mean by that?'

'It's not true because she's never poorly.'

A hand hastily laid itself on my head as if the tiles were about to fall from the roof.

'Don't change the subject. What am I going to do with this moth-eaten cloak? Such a big cloak, too! Five metres long at the very least!'

'Good Heavens, my dear, if you're so very bothered about it, fold it up again, pin its little shroud round it, and put it back in the cupboard – just as if it had never been eaten by moths!'

The blood rose into her still-fresh cheeks, as quickly as it always did.

'Oh, but you can't be serious! It's not the same thing at all! I just couldn't. It's almost a question of...'

'All right then, my dear, give the cloak to me. I've had an idea.'

'What are you going to do with it?'

'Leave it with me. I've had an idea, I said.'

She gave him the cloak, all her habitual trust shining in her grey eyes. Hadn't he informed her successively that he knew how to make a certain type of chocolate caramel, how to save half the corks when bottling a cask of Bordeaux, and how to kill off the mole-crickets that were ravaging our lettuces? The fact that the badly corked wine had spoiled within six months, that making the caramels had led to a fire, a metre of parquet being burnt, and a complete suit of clothes crystallised in the boiling sugar, and that the lettuces, poisoned by some mysterious acid, had gone to their graves rather sooner than the mole-crickets – none of this meant that my father had actually made a mistake...

She gave him the spahi's cloak, and he flung it across his shoulders and carried off into his lair, also known as his library. I followed his one leg clumping quickly upstairs as he hoisted himself up from step to step like a hopping crow. But in the library he sat down, tersely asked me to bring him his slide rule, his glue, the big pair of scissors, a pair of compasses and some pins, then sent me away and bolted the door behind him.

'What's he doing? Just pop up and see what he's doing!' my mother kept asking.

We didn't find out until the evening. Finally, my father's loud, clear voice echoed all the way down to us, and we went upstairs.

'Well,' said my mother, 'successful?'

'Look!'

With an air of triumph, he held out to her on the palm of his hand – cut into a wolf's-teeth pattern, foliated like a girdle-cake, and no bigger than a rose – all that was left of the spahi's cloak: a very attractive pen-wiper.

The Friend

The day the Opéra-Comique burnt down, my elder brother, together with another student, his best friend, had wanted to book two seats. But other impecunious music-lovers, used to buying up all the three-franc seats, had taken everything. The two disappointed students had dinner outside a little restaurant in the district: one hour later, two hundred metres away from them, the Opéra-Comique was ablaze. Before running off, one to send a reassuring telegram to my mother, and the other to alert his family in Paris, they both shook hands and gazed at each other with that embarrassment and awkwardness behind which very young men disguise the purity of their emotions. Neither of them mentioned the providential good luck or the mysterious protection that had been extended over their heads. But when the summer holidays came, for the first time Maurice – let's just say he was called Maurice – came home with my brother to spend two months with us.

I was then quite a big little girl, about thirteen.

So there he was, that Maurice whom I blindly admired on the basis of my brother's friendship for him. In two years, I had learnt that Maurice was studying law – for me, this was rather as if someone had said he was learning how to 'sit up on his hind legs and beg'; he loved music just as much as did my brother; he looked like the baritone Taskin[46] with his moustache and a very small pointy beard; his rich parents sold chemical products wholesale and earned at least fifty thousand francs a year – as you can see, it was all a long time ago.

There he was, and my mother immediately exclaimed that he was 'a thousand times' better than his photos, and even better than the flattering picture my brother had been painting of him for the past two years: elegant, with velvety eyes, nice hands, a moustache that looked as if it had been singed in the fire, and the ease of manner of a son who has rarely left his mother's side. I myself said nothing – after all, I shared my mother's enthusiasm.

When he arrived he was dressed in blue, and on his head there sat a panama with a striped ribbon; he brought me some sweets, chenille monkeys in garnet, old gold and peacock-green – it was the irritating fashion to hang them everywhere; they were the Rin-Tin-Tins[47] of the day – and a little purse in turquoise plush. But what were these presents worth in comparison with my petty thefts? I stole from him and my brother anything I could get my sentimental little magpie claws on: risqué magazines, cigarettes from the East, cough drops, a pencil with tooth-marks at one end – and above all, empty matchboxes, those new boxes emblazoned with the photos of actresses, all of whom I soon got to know and to identify unerringly: Théo, Sybil Sanderson, Van Zandt... They belonged to an unknown, admirable race which nature had invariably endowed with huge eyes, intensely black eyelashes, hair curled in a fringe on the forehead, and a band of tulle over one shoulder, while the other shoulder was bare... Hearing Maurice casually naming them, I assembled them all into a harem over which he extended his indolent sovereignty, and when I went to bed each night, I would try out one of Maman's veils on my shoulder. For a whole week I was crabby, jealous, pale, flushed – in a word, in love.

And then, as I was, basically, a perfectly sensible little girl, this period of exultation faded away and I started to enjoy Maurice's friendship and cheerful good humour to the full, as well as the way the two friends would chat away to their hearts' content. A more intelligent coquetry now governed my every movement, and, although I apparently shunned any sophistication, I became the person I needed to be if I were to please others: a tall girl with long braids, my waist tightly encircled by a ribbon with a bow, as watchful as a cat under her great straw hat. I could be found in the kitchen with my hands in the dough for the cakes, in the garden with my foot on the spade, and I tagged along with the two friends like a graceful and faithful guardian angel when, arm in arm, they went out for a walk. What sun-filled holidays they were, so intense and pure…

It was while listening to the two young men talking together that I learnt of Maurice's forthcoming marriage, still some way off. One day when we were alone in the garden, I grew bold enough to ask him for a portrait of his fiancée. He held it out for me to see: she was a smiling young girl, pretty, with her hair done up very elegantly, and ensconced in a thousand ruches of lace.

'Oh!' I said, stuck for words, 'what a lovely dress!'

He laughed so openly that I didn't apologise.

'And what are you going to do once you're married?' I asked.

He stopped laughing and gazed at me.

'What do you mean – what am I going to do? I'm already practically a lawyer, you know!'

'I know. But what about your fiancée – what will she do while you're being a lawyer?'

'How funny you are! She'll be my wife, of course.'

'Will she put on other dresses with lots of little ruches?'

'She'll look after our house, she'll invite people round… Are you pulling my leg? You know perfectly well what people do when they're married.'

'No, not really. But I know how we've been living for the past month and a half.'

'Who do you mean – "we"?'

'You, my brother and me. Do you like it here? Have you been happy? Do you like us?'

He raised his dark eyes to the slate roof embroidered with yellow, to the wisteria in its second bloom, then rested them for a moment on me and replied, as if talking to himself, 'But of course…'

'After, when you're married, I suppose you won't be able to come back here to spend your holidays? You won't ever be able to go out for a walk at my brother's side, holding my two braids at the end, like reins?'

I was trembling all over, but I didn't take my eyes off him. Something changed in his expression. He looked all around, then he seemed to measure, from head to foot, the little girl leaning against a tree and lifting her head to talk to him, since she still hadn't grown as tall as he was. I remember that he forced out a half-smile, then shrugged, and replied, rather foolishly, 'Good Lord, no, of course not...'

He moved off towards the house without adding a word, and for the first time I found that the huge sense of childish regret I felt at the imminent loss of Maurice was mingled with the muted but victorious sorrow of a grown woman.

Ybañez is Dead

I've forgotten his name. Why does his sorrowful face still emerge, at times, from the dreams that at night take me back to the time and place where I spent my childhood? Does his sorrowful face drift around in the place where dwell those dead who have no friends, after drifting around, without friends, among the living?

His name was something like Goussard or Voussard, or perhaps Gaumeau. He entered the practice of Maître Defert, the notary, as a forwarding clerk, and he stayed there for years and years… But my village, which was not the birthplace of this Voussard – or Gaumeau – was unwilling to adopt him. Even seniority did not enable Voussard to achieve the status of 'one of us'. Tall, grey, thin, bony, he sought no one's friendship, and even Rouillard's heart – the expansive heart of a café proprietor and violinist, which had grown tender by dint of leading the music for wedding processions along the roads – never opened up to him.

Voussard used to 'eat' at Patasson's. 'To eat at so-and-so's' means, in our part of the world, that you live there too. Sixty francs a month for full board and lodging: Voussard was in no danger of getting fat, and his figure continued to be skinny, trussed up in a shiny jacket and a yellow waistcoat darned with coarse black thread. Yes, darned with coarse thread… just above the pocket where he kept his watch… I can see it now… If I were a painter, I'd be able to produce an astonishingly life-like portrait of Voussard, twenty-five years after his death. Why? I don't know. That waistcoat, the black thread darning, the white cardboard collar, and the cravat, a ragged thing with a Paisley pattern. Over it hung his face, in the morning as grey as a dirty window pane, since Voussard always set off without having breakfasted, and after the midday meal blotched with pale red patches. His face was long; he never wore a beard but he was always ill-shaven. A big mouth, tight-lipped and ugly. A long nose, an avid nose, thicker than his whole face, and eyes... I only ever saw them once, since they usually stared at the ground and were in any case sheltered under a black straw boater, too small for Voussard's skull and pulled over his forehead like the hats worn by women during the Second Empire, when it was fashionable to have your hair done in a Benoîton[48] bun.

When the time came for after-dinner liqueurs and cigarettes, Voussard, who never indulged in coffee or tobacco, would take the air a few feet away from his office, on one of the two stone benches that must still flank Mme Lachassagne's house. He would return here at around four o'clock, the time when the rest of the village was having its late afternoon snack. The bench on the left wore out the trouser seats of Maître Defert's two clerks. When the weather was fine, at the same hours the bench on the right would be wobbling under the weight of a serried row of already quite grown-up little girls, packed together and as fidgety as sparrows on the ledge of a hot chimney: Odile, Yvonne, Marie, Colette... We were thirteen or fourteen years old: the age of the premature chignon, the leather belt buckled up tight to the last hole, the shoes that pinch, the straight fringe, which – 'Maman can say what she likes, I don't care!' – was cut that way at school, during the sewing lesson, with a pair of embroidery scissors. We were slim, sunburnt, affected and brutal, as clumsy as boys, impudent, blushing for shyness at the mere sound of our own voices, shrill, full of grace, insufferable...

For a few minutes, sitting on the bench before school, we used to preen ourselves for the sake of everything on two legs that came down from the heights of Bel-Air; but we never spared a glance for Voussard, who sat hunched over a newspaper folded into eight. Our mothers were vaguely afraid of him.

'You haven't been sitting on that bench again, right next to that fellow?'

'Which fellow, Maman?'

'That fellow from Defert's... I really don't like you doing that!'

'Why ever not, Maman?'

'I know what I mean...'

They felt for him the same horror that people feel for satyrs, or the silent madman who suddenly commits a murder. But Voussard seemed unaware of our presence and we hardly even considered him to be alive.

He used to chew on the twig of a lime tree in place of dessert; he crossed his fleshless shins with the casual gesture of a frivolous skeleton, and sat there reading, under the awning of his dusty straw hat. At half-past twelve, young Ménétreau, who the year before had been a mere school-kid and had recently been promoted to the job of errand boy at Defert's, was sitting next to Voussard, his teeth tearing into his midday hunk of bread, like a fox terrier tearing a slipper to pieces. Mme Lachassagne's flower-covered wall sprinkled them, and us, with wisteria, laburnum, the scent of lime, the flat corolla of a clematis spinning downwards, red yew-berries... Odile feigned an outburst of hysterical laughter so as to attract the admiration of a travelling salesman who happened to be passing by; Yvonne was waiting for the new assistant teacher to appear at the window of the upper-form classroom; I was planning to put my piano out of tune, so that the local piano-tuner, the one who wore a gold pince-nez... Voussard, as if inanimate, sat reading.

One day, young Ménétreau was the first to sit on the left side of the bench, munching what was left of his bread and filling his mouth with cherries. Voussard arrived late, just as the school-bell was ringing. He was walking hastily and awkwardly, like someone hurrying through the dark. An open newspaper that he was holding was trailing along in the street. He placed a hand on young Ménétreau's shoulder, bent over and told him in grave but rapid tones:

'Ybañez is dead. They've murdered him.'[49]

Young Ménétreau opened a mouth crammed with masticated bread and stammered:

'What – are you sure?'

'Yes. The king's soldiers. Look.'

And with a tragic flourish, his fingers trembling, he unfolded the newspaper right under the nose of the errand boy, and showed him the story.

'Oh dear!...' sighed young Ménétreau. 'What's going to happen now?'

'Ah!... If only I knew!...'

Voussard's long arms rose and fell.

'It's that Cardinal Richelieu that's behind it,' he added, with a bitter laugh.

Then he took off his hat to mop his brow and stood there motionless for a few moments, as his eyes that we had never really seen wandered across the valley – the yellow eyes of a conqueror of islands, the cruel and far-seeing eyes of a pirate keeping a lookout from under his black flag, the desperate eyes of the loyal companion of Ybañez, murdered in cowardly fashion by 'His Majestie's Men'.

My Mother and the Priest

My mother was an unbeliever, but she allowed me to take catechism lessons when I was eleven or twelve. The only obstacle she ever put in my way consisted of the disparaging remarks, robustly expressed, that she uttered every time a humble little book bound in blue boards fell into her hands. She would open my catechism at random and immediately lose her temper.

'Oh I really *hate* this way of asking questions! What is God? What is this? What is that? These question marks, this obsession with inquiry and inquisition – I find it insufferably prying! And as for those commandments – well! Whoever translated the commandments into such gibberish? I don't like seeing this book in a child's hands, it's full of such far-fetched and complicated things…'

'Then take it out of your daughter's hands,' said my father. 'It's perfectly simple.'

'No, it's not perfectly simple. If it was just the catechism! But there's confession as well. That – well… that really takes the biscuit! I can't even talk about it without turning red with indignation… Look how red I've gone!'

'Then stop talking about it.'

'Oh, *you*!… It's your outlook that's "perfectly simple". If things bother you, don't talk about them, and they'll go away – is that it?'

'I couldn't have put it better myself.'

'Joke all you like, but that's still not an answer. I just can't get used to the questions they ask this girl.'

'!!!'

'It's all very well you throwing up your arms! Having to reveal and confess and confess again, and make an exhibition of all the wrong you've done!… You should keep it quiet and punish yourself for it inside yourself – that's a much better idea.

That's what they ought to be teaching them. But confession makes children inclined to talk and talk and indulge in nitpicking self-analysis – they soon start to take a conceited pleasure in it, rather than developing a sense of humility... Let me tell you, I'm really vexed! And I'm going round to speak to the priest about it right now!'

She flung round her shoulders her pelisse in black cashmere with jet embroidery, put on her small coif with its bunches of purple lilac, and did indeed set off, 'right now', with her inimitable, dancing step – the point of her foot turned outwards, the heel scarcely skimming the ground – to ring the doorbell of Father Millot, who lived a hundred metres away. I could hear from our house the melancholy, crystal-clear ringing of the bell, and in my troubled imagination I could hear a dramatic conversation, threats and invectives, between my mother and the parish priest... When I heard the front door slamming shut, my fanciful child's heart responded by lurching painfully. My mother reappeared looking radiant, and my father lowered his copy of *Le Temps* newspaper in front of his face, as bearded as a forested landscape.

'Well?'

'Done it!' exclaimed my mother. 'I've got what I wanted!'

'The priest?'

'No! What are you thinking of? The pelargonium cutting he has been guarding so jealously – you know, the one whose flowers have two deep-purple petals and three pink ones? Here it is; I need to get it straight into a pot...'

'Did you give him a good telling-off about the girl, then?'

My mother, on the threshold of the terrace, turned her charming, astonished, flushed face.

'Of course not! What an idea! You have no sense of tact! A man who's not only given me his pelargonium cutting, but has promised me his Spanish honeysuckle with little variegated white leaves – you can catch its scent from here, you know, when the wind's in the west…'

She was already out of sight, but her voice was still audible, a modulated soprano that trembled whenever she felt the least emotion, an agile voice that broadcast to us – and further afield as well – the news it brought of plants she was tending, of grafts, rain-showers and new blooms, like the voice of an invisible bird predicting the weather…

On Sundays, she rarely missed Mass. In winter, she took her foot-warmer with her; in summer, her parasol; in all seasons, a big black prayer-book and her dog Domino, who took the shape, successively, of a black and white mongrel offspring of a spitz and a fox terrier, and then a yellow water spaniel.

Old Father Millot, although almost won over by my mother's voice, imperious kindness and scandalous sincerity, pointed out that Mass was not for dogs.

She bristled like a belligerent hen.

'My dog! You want to throw my dog out of church? What are you frightened he might learn there?'

'It's not a question of…'

'A dog who is a model of decorum! A dog who stands up and sits down at the same time as the rest of your flock!'

'My dear Madame, all of that is true. Nonetheless, last Sunday, he growled during the Elevation!'

'But of course he growled during the Elevation! I'd like to know why he *shouldn't* growl during the Elevation! A dog I myself trained to keep guard, and who knows he has to growl the minute he hears a bell ring!'

The case of the churchgoing dog, interrupted by periods of truce and punctuated by sudden flare-ups, lasted a long time, but the victory fell to my mother. At eleven o'clock, flanked by her dog – who was actually very well behaved – she would shut herself into the family pew, just beneath the pulpit, with the somewhat forced and puerile gravity that she assumed as her Sunday best. The holy water, the sign of the cross – she forgot nothing, not even the ritual genuflections.

'What do you know about whether I pray or not, Father? I don't know my paternoster, that's true. It doesn't take long to learn, you say? No, and it doesn't take long to forget, as I soon would… But at Mass, when you make us go down on our knees, I have two or three nice quiet moments when I can think over a few problems… I tell myself that Little One doesn't look very well, that I'll have a bottle of Château Larose sent up to her so she doesn't get pasty-faced… Then at the Pluviers', poor folk, there's another child coming into the world without nappies or vests, unless I take things in hand… And then tomorrow it's washing day at home and I have to get up at four o'clock…'

He stopped her, holding out his sunburnt gardener's hand.

'That's enough, that's quite enough… As far as I'm concerned, it all counts as a kind of prayer.'

During Mass, she would read a book bound in black leather, with a cross stamped on it back and front; she even became absorbed in it, with a piety that seemed strange to the friends of my darling unbeliever; they could never have guessed that, behind the appearance of a prayer-book, it concealed a pocket-book edition of Corneille's plays…

But when the time came for the sermon, my mother was transformed into a she-devil. The rustic pronunciation, the naive Christianity of an old country priest – nothing would reconcile her to it. Nervous yawns escaped from her like flames; and she murmured into my ear the countless ills that were suddenly assailing her.

'My stomach's really out of sorts… Oh no, I can sense an attack of palpitations coming on… I'm flushed, aren't I? I think I'm going to be sick… I must forbid Father Millot from giving sermons that last longer than ten minutes…'

She communicated her latest ukase to him, and this time he told her where to get off. But the following Sunday, once the sermon had overstepped the ten-minute mark, she contrived to cough, let her book drop to the floor and swing her watch ostentatiously at the end of its chain...

The priest struggled on for a while, but then lost his head and the thread of what he was saying. He stammered out a premature 'Amen' and descended, distractedly blessing his faithful flock – all his faithful flock, not excepting the one whose face, level with his feet, was laughing and gleaming with all the insolence of the reprobate.

My Mother and Morals

At around the age of thirteen or fourteen, I was not particularly fond of social life. My elder half-brother, who was studying medicine, used to instil in me, whenever he came home for the holidays, his own serene and methodical antisocial tendencies, which were as unremitting as the vigilance of wild animals. If the front doorbell rang, it would propel him with a single silent bound into the garden, and the huge house, in bad weather, offered many a refuge to the delights of solitude. By imitation or instinct, I knew how to jump through the kitchen window, climb over the spiked railings on the rue des Vignes, and melt away into the shadow of the lofts, the minute I heard, straight after the ring of the doorbell, the sound of friendly feminine voices, speaking in the sing-song accent of our province. All the same, I enjoyed the visits of Mme Saint-Alban, a still handsome woman, with naturally curly hair which she wore parted down the middle and was prone to getting dishevelled. She resembled George Sand, and all her movements were imbued with a certain gypsy-like majesty. Her warm yellow eyes reflected the sun and the green plants, and while still a nursling child, I had drunk the milk of her generous and swarthy breast, one day when, as a joke, my mother proffered her white breast to a little Saint-Alban boy the same age as me.

When she came to see my mother, Mme Saint-Alban would leave her house on the street corner and her narrow garden where the pallor of the clematis stood out in the shadow of the thujas. Or else she would call in on her way back from a walk, laden down with wild honeysuckle, purple heather, water-mint and flowering reeds, velvety, brown and rough as the backs of bear cubs. She often used her oval brooch to pin together the edges of a tear in her black taffeta dress, and her little finger bore a heart-shaped pink cornelian, where the words 'I burne,

I burne' gleamed like flames – it was an antique ring she had picked up in the fields.

I think that what I most liked about Mme Saint-Alban was everything that set her apart from my mother, and, with a reflective sensuality, I would breathe in their mingled perfumes. From Mme Saint-Alban there wafted a heavy, tawny aroma, the incense of her curly hair and her golden arms. My mother gave off a bloom of freshly washed cretonne, the iron heated on the poplar-log brazier and the leaves of lemon verbena that she rolled in her hands or crushed in her pocket. As dusk fell, I thought that she emitted the odour of recently watered lettuces, since their fresh smell rose from her footprints, accompanied by the ripple of the drops from the watering can, in a glory of water spray and arable dust.

I also enjoyed hearing the communal chronicle as related by Mme Saint-Alban. Her tales would leave a sort of blazon of disaster hanging from each familiar name – a weather forecast in which tomorrow's adultery, next week's ruined family, or some incurable illness were all foretold... On these occasions, a noble flame would illuminate her yellow eyes, and she would be filled with an enthusiastic if diffuse malevolence, and I had to restrain myself from crying, 'Encore! Encore!'

In my presence she would sometimes lower her voice. The mysterious piece of gossip, all the more alluring for being only half-understood, lasted for several days, a fire skilfully stirred and then suddenly extinguished. I remember in particular the 'Bonnarjaud story'...

M. and Mme de Bonnarjaud, the possessors of an imaginary baronetcy or some rustic titles of nobility, led an austere life in a little chateau around which their domains, having been sold off piecemeal, had been reduced to a park enclosed by walls. They had no fortune, and three daughters to marry off. 'Those Bonnarjaud girls' wore revealing dresses when they went to Mass. Would those Bonnarjaud girls ever be married off?…

'Sido? Guess what's happened!' exclaimed Mme Saint-Alban one day. 'The second Bonnarjaud girl is getting married!'

She was on her way home from the farms scattered around the little chateau, bearing her booty of news and swathes of unripe oats, poppies and corn-cockles, and the first foxgloves from the stony ravines. A spinning caterpillar, the colour of transparent jade, hung by a silky thread from Mme Saint-Alban's ear; the down of the poplars had stuck a silver beard to her copper-coloured chin with its sheen of sweat.

'Sit down, Adrienne. You can have a glass of my redcurrant syrup. As you can see, I'm tying up my nasturtiums. The second Bonnarjaud girl? The one who limps a bit? I sense someone's been pulling strings behind the scenes… But the life those three girls lead – it's so sad and empty it wrings your heart. Boredom is so corrupting! What morals can hold out against boredom?'

'Oh dear, if you're going to start talking morals, we could be here for ever! Anyway, it's not an absurd marriage. She's marrying… oh, you'll never guess! Gaillard du Gougier!'

My mother was far from impressed. She pursed her lips.

'Gaillard du Gougier! Really? A nice catch, to be sure!'

'The handsomest bachelor in the region! All the marriageable girls are crazy about him.'

'Why "about him"? Just say, "All marriageable girls are crazy." Anyway… when's the wedding?'

'Ah! There's the rub!…'

'I thought there'd be a problem somewhere!…'

'The Bonnarjauds are waiting for a great-aunt to die: her whole fortune will go to the girls. If the aunt dies, they'll be able to aim higher than young Gougier – no doubt about it! That's how it stands…'

The following week, we learnt that the Gougiers and the Bonnarjauds were 'giving each other the cold shoulder'. A month later, once the great-aunt had died, the Baron de Bonnarjaud threw Gougier out 'as if he'd been a lackey'. Finally, towards the end of summer, Mme Saint-Alban, like some gypsy Pomona, trailing garlands of red vines and bunches of meadow saffron, came over in a great tizzy and murmured into my mother's ear a few words that I didn't catch.

'No! Really?' my mother exclaimed.

Then she flushed red with indignation.

'What are they going to do?' she asked, after a silence.

Mme Saint-Alban shrugged her lovely shoulders draped with wild clematis.

'What do you mean, "what are they going to do"? Marry them off in five seconds, of course! What else could they do, those fine folk the Bonnarjauds? The deed was already done three months ago, apparently. It seems that Gaillard du Gougier used to meet the girl in the evening, right next to the house, in the pavilion that...'

'And Madame de Bonnarjaud is giving him her daughter?'

Mme Saint-Alban laughed like a Bacchante.

'Good Lord! You bet! And she's only too glad to do so, I'll be bound! So what would you do in her place?'

My mother's grey eyes turned to me, and rested on me sternly.

'What would I do? I would say to my daughter, "Bear your burden, my daughter, and go, not far from me but far from that man, and never see him again! Or, if the base desire to see him again still holds you in its thrall, meet him at night, in the pavilion. Hide your shameful pleasure. But don't let that man cross the threshold in broad daylight, since he has shown himself capable of taking you in the shadows, under the windows of your sleeping parents. To sin and then to kick yourself for it, to sin and then to drive the unworthy man away, means that your shame is not irreparable. Your ruin begins the minute you agree to become the wife of a dishonest man, and your mistake lies in hoping that such a man can give you any home that will replace the home from which he has stolen you away.'

Laughter

She liked to laugh, and had a youthful, shrill laugh that brought tears to her eyes, for which she would afterwards reproach herself, as being unworthy of the dignity of a mother with four children to look after and money troubles as well. She would bring her ripples of mirth under control, and give herself a good scolding – 'Now then! That's enough!' – only to relapse into another fit of laughter that made her pince-nez tremble.

We would compete to see who could set her off laughing, especially when we turned old enough to see how, year by year, her face expressed an increasing care for the morrow, a sort of dismay that overshadowed her whenever her thoughts turned to the fate of her penniless children, her precarious health, and the old age that was slowing down her beloved companion on his single leg and two crutches. When she stayed silent, my mother resembled all mothers who are filled with alarm at the prospect of poverty and death. But when she spoke, her face was again flooded by an invincible, youthful light. Even though she grew thin with sorrow, her voice was never despondent. She would come out of some painful reverie as if in a single bound, and exclaim, as she pointed her knitting needle at her husband:

'Oh yes? Well just you try and die before me. You'll see!'

'I'll do my best, my love,' he would reply.

She stared at him as ferociously as if he had absent-mindedly crushed a pelargonium cutting or smashed the little Chinese teapot with its golden niello work.

'That's just you all over, that is! All the selfishness of the Funels and the Colettes combined! Oh, why did I ever marry you?'

'My love, it's because I threatened to blow your brains out if you didn't.'

'That's true. You see? Already in those days all you co∖ think of was yourself. And now you're even talking of dying before me. Go on then! Just try!…'

He tried, and succeeded at the first attempt. He died in his seventy-fourth year, holding the hands of his beloved wife, and fixing on her tear-filled eyes a gaze that gradually lost its colour, turning a hazy, milky blue, as pale as a sky covered by the mist. He had the most splendid funeral in a village cemetery, a coffin of yellow wood, quite bare under an old tunic pierced with wounds – the tunic he had worn as a captain in the First Zouaves – and my mother accompanied him to the tomb without stumbling, small and resolute under her veils, and murmuring quiet words of love, just for him to hear.

We brought her back to the house, where she rebelled against her new mourning apparel, the heavy, awkward crape that she kept snagging on all the keys in all the drawers and doors, and the cashmere dress that was suffocating her.

She rested in the living room, near the big green armchair where my father would never sit again and which the dog had already taken the greatest pleasure in occupying. She was feverish, flushed in the face, and kept saying, dry-eyed:

'Oh, it's so hot! My God, these black clothes make you feel so hot! Don't you think that now I can put my blue sateen dress back on?'

'But…'

'What's that? Because I'm in mourning? But I hate wearing this black! To begin with it's depressing. Why do you think I should present such a gloomy, dismal spectacle to the people I meet? What do this cashmere and crape have to do with my feelings? Just let me see *you* wearing mourning like this! You know perfectly well that the only colours I like on you are pink, and certain shades of blue…'

ruptly to her feet, and took a few steps towards an
m. Then she stopped.

rue...'

came back to the chair, with a humble and simple gesture
admitting that she had just – for the first time all day – forgotten
that *he* was dead.

'Would you like me to get you a drink, Maman? Wouldn't
you like to go to bed?'

'No! Why should I? I'm not ill!'

She sat down again, and started to learn the art of patience,
gazing at the parquet floor where, from the door of the living
room to the door of the empty bedroom, there was a dusty trail
marked by heavy, coarse shoes.

A little cat came in, circumspect and naive, an ordinary and
irresistible kitten four to five months old. He was acting out for
himself some majestic drama, with measured steps and his tail
held high like a candle, imitating the lordly tomcats. But a
daring and unexpected somersault flung him head over heels at
our feet, where he was filled with alarm at his own extravagance, and rolled himself up into a turban, stood up on his hind
legs, danced sideways, arched his back and changed himself into
a spinning top...

'Look, just look at him, Little-Darling! My God, how funny
he is!'

And she started laughing, my mother in mourning, laughing
her shrill, girlish laugh and clapping her hands at the sight of the
little cat... The flickering stab of memory choked that brilliant
ripple and wiped the tears of laughter from my mother's eyes.
All the same, she made no apology for having laughed, either
that day or on the following days, since, having lost the man she
had loved deeply and truly, she was graceful enough to remain
in our presence the woman she had always been, accepting her
sorrow in exactly the same way she would have accepted the

start of a long, gloomy season in the calendar, but receiving from all sides the fleeting blessings of joy. She continued to live a life swept by darkness and light, bowed under her torments, resigned, changeable in mood and generous, as rich in children, flowers and animals as some fertile kingdom.

My Mother and Illness

'What's the time? Eleven o'clock already! You see! He'll be here any minute. Give me the eau de Cologne and the towel sponge. And give me the little bottle of violet scent too. And when I say violet… There isn't any real violet scent any more. They make it with orris root. Come to think of it, do they even make it with orris root? Still, you don't care either way, do you Little-Darling? You don't like essence of violet. Whatever is wrong with our girls these days – they don't even like violet any more!

'In days gone by, a really distinguished woman would never wear any scent other than violet. That perfume you drench yourself in really isn't suitable. You use it to delude people. Oh yes you do – you delude them! Your short hair, the blue you put on your eyelids, those eccentricities you indulge in when you're on the stage – it's all just like the perfume you wear, it's meant to delude people. Oh yes it is: it's so that people will think you're original and emancipated, that you've shed all your prejudices… Poor Little-Darling! *I* won't fall for that trick!… Undo my two wretched little plaits, I did them up tight last night so I'd have a wave this morning. Do you know what I look like? Like a poet without talent, aged and needy. It's rather difficult to preserve the characteristics of one's sex after a certain age. There are two things that I really regret as I go from bad to worse: not being able to wash my little blue saucepan for boiling milk in any more, and looking at my hand as it rests on the sheet. You'll come to realise later that we continually forget old age until we've got one foot in the grave.

'Not even illness can make you remember it. I keep telling myself, "My back aches. My neck aches dreadfully. I don't have any appetite. Digitalis makes me feel woozy and sick! I'm going to die: this evening, tomorrow, it hardly matters…" But I don't always think of the changes that age has inflicted on me. And it's when I look at my hand that I can measure these changes. I'm amazed that I don't see before me the slender little hand I had at the age of twenty… Sshh! Hush a minute, I want to listen. I can hear singing… Ah, they're burying old Madame Loeuvrier. What a good thing it is they're finally burying her! No, I'm not being cruel! I say "a good thing" because it'll stop her bothering her poor idiot of a daughter, who's fifty-five and has never dared to get married because she was afraid of her mother. Ah, parents! I say "a good thing" because it's a good thing there's one old woman less on the earth…

'No, there's no denying it, I just can't get used to old age, neither mine nor other people's. And since I'm seventy-one, I may as well give up the attempt: I'll never get used to it. Be a sweetheart, Little-Darling, and push my bed over to the window so I can see old Madame Loeuvrier go by. I love watching funeral processions go by, you always learn something. What a lot of people! That's because of the fine weather. It makes it a nice little excursion for them. If it was raining, she'd have just had three cats to see her off, and Monsieur Miroux wouldn't deign to get his lovely black and silver cope all wet. And so many flowers! Ah, the vandals! The whole saffron rose tree in the Loeuvriers' garden has been cut down. For such an old lady, killing off all those young flowers…

'And look, look at her great idiot of a daughter: I was sure of it, she's crying her eyes out. Still, it's logical enough: she's lost her torturer, her tormenter, her daily dose of poison – maybe the deprivation will kill her. Behind her come the coffin-chasers as I call them, with their ugly mugs. Just look at their faces! There are days when I congratulate myself I won't be leaving you a brass farthing. The idea that I might be followed to my final resting place by a red-headed lad like that, the nephew, see him? – the one who's going to spend every minute from now on waiting for the daughter to die… Brrr!

'You lot at least, I know you, you'll miss me. Who will you write to twice a week, my poor Little-Darling? And you're all right, you've broken away and made a nest for yourself, far from me. But what about your elder brother? He's going to have to walk straight past my house when he comes back from his rounds, and he won't find his glass of redcurrant juice waiting for him and the rose he puts between his teeth... Yes, yes, *you* love me, but you're a girl, the female of the species, my equal and my rival. But I've always been without a female rival in *his* heart. Does my hair look all right? No, no cap, just my Spanish lace kerchief, he'll be here any minute. All that crowd of people in black have kicked up a dust, I can hardly breathe.

'It's nearly midday, isn't it? If nobody's stopped him en route, your brother must be less than a league away. Open the door for the cat, she knows that it's nearly midday too. Every day she's afraid, after her morning walk, that she'll come back and find me cured. Now she can sleep on my bed night and day – it's the life of Riley for her!... Your brother was supposed to go to Arnedon and Coulefeuilles this morning, and come back by way of Saint-André. I never forget his schedule. I follow him, you know. In Arnedon he's looking after the son of the lovely Arthémise. Those love-children always suffer because their mothers try to conceal them under a tight-fitting corset: they get crushed. It's a shame – after all, it's not such a scandalous thing to see a lovely impenitent girl with a cargo in her belly...

'Listen, listen... There's the trap just coming over the hill! Little-Darling, don't tell your brother that I had three attacks last night. For one thing, I forbid you to. And if you don't tell him, I'll give you the bracelet with the three turquoises... Don't be such a bore, with all your arguments. It's nothing to do with observing the decencies! For one thing, I know better than you what being decent means. But at my age there's only one virtue left: not causing a fuss. Quick, put the second pillow behind my back, so I can be sitting upright when he comes in. The two roses over there, in that glass… It doesn't smell too much like an old lady's stuffy room in here, does it? Is my face flushed? He's going to think I don't look as well as I did yesterday, I shouldn't have rabbited on for so long, that's true… Close the shutter a bit, and then listen, Little-Darling, do just lend me your powder puff…'

My Mother and the Forbidden Fruit

The time came when her strength abandoned her. This filled her with boundless astonishment, and she refused to believe it. Every time I came from Paris to see her, she always had some peccadillo to confess to me as soon as we were alone in the little house after lunch. On one occasion, she hitched up the hem of her dress, rolled down her stocking over her shin, and showed me a purple bruise where the skin had almost been torn.

'Just take a look at that!'

'Now what have you gone and done to yourself, Maman?'

She opened her eyes wide: they were filled with innocence and confusion.

'You'd never believe it: I fell down the stairs!'

'How do you mean, you fell?'

'That's just it – I don't really know! I was coming down the stairs and I fell. I've no idea why.'

'Were you coming down too quickly?'

'Too quickly? What do you mean by too quickly? I was coming down quickly. Do I have time to come down stairs as slowly as the Sun King? And that's not all… just look at this!'

On her pretty arm, still so young in contrast to her withered hand, there was a big blister from a scald.

'And what's that then?'

'My kettle.'

'The old copper kettle? The one that can hold five litres?'

'Yes, that one. Who can you trust? She's known me for forty years. I don't know what came over her, she was bubbling and boiling away, I went to take her off the fire when bang! – something gave in my wrist… I'm fortunate I got off with nothing worse than that blister… But just fancy that! Anyway, I left the cupboard alone…'

She blushed bright red and didn't complete her sentence.

'What cupboard?' I asked sternly.

My mother wriggled and writhed, shaking her head as though I wanted to put her on a leash.

'Nothing! No cupboard at all!'

'Maman! You'll make me get cross!'

'Listen, I said "I left the cupboard alone," so you can do as much for me. That old cupboard hasn't budged from its place, all right? So just leave me alone, all of you!'

The cupboard... an edifice in old walnut, almost as broad as it is high, without any carving except the neat round hole left by a Prussian bullet that went in by the right-hand door and came out by the back panel... Hmmm!...

'Would you like it to be moved away from the landing, Maman?'

She glanced at me like a young cat, her eyes filled with a mendacious twinkle in her wrinkled face.

'Who, me? No, I think it's fine there: it can stay!'

Still, my brother, the doctor and I agreed that caution was needed. He saw my mother every day, since she had followed him to live in the same village; he looked after her with a secret passion. She struggled against all her ailments with a surprising resilience: she forgot them, tricked them, and won fleeting but dazzling victories over them, summoning up her vanished strength for days on end; and the noise of her battles, whenever I spent a few days with her, could be heard throughout the little house, reminding me of a fox terrier worrying a rat...

At five o'clock in the morning, opposite my bedroom, the chiming of the full bucket being placed on the kitchen sink would ring out and wake me...

'What are you doing with the bucket, Maman? Can't you wait till Joséphine arrives?'

I ran down. But the fire was already blazing, fed with dry sticks of wood. The milk was boiling on the charcoal stove with its blue faience tiles. There was also a bar of chocolate for my breakfast melting in a couple of inches of water. My mother, securely installed in her cane armchair, was grinding the fragrant coffee, which she roasted herself. The morning hours were always kind to her; she wore their bright red colours in her cheeks. Her complexion briefly glowed with health again in the light of the rising sun, and as the church bell chimed for the first Mass of the day, she rejoiced at having already enjoyed, while we slept, so many forbidden fruits.

These forbidden fruits were the bucket that was too heavy for her but that she hauled up from the well; the wood for kindling she had split with a billhook on a block of oak wood; the spade; the mattock; and in particular the stepladder propped against the gable window of the wood-house. They were the climbing vine whose shoots she trained up to the gable window of the attic, the flowering spikes of the lilac that grew too high, the cat that had climbed onto the rooftop and succumbed to an attack of vertigo and needed to be rescued... All the accomplices of this plump, sturdy little woman's life, all the subaltern rustic divinities that had obeyed her and made her so proud that she could manage without servants now assumed the shape and posture of adversaries. But they hadn't reckoned with the pleasure my mother took in putting up a fight, which would not leave her until the day she died. At the age of seventy-one, each day dawned to see her bloodied but unbowed. She had burnt herself, cut herself on the billhook, drenched herself in melted snow or spilt water, but she still found a means to live to the full her finest and most independent hours before even the earliest risers had opened their shutters, and she could tell us all about the cats awakening, the birds busy in their nests, all the news that the milkmaid and the baker's girl had brought along with the daily milk and warm loaf of bread – in short, the chronicle of the new day's birth.

It was only when I saw, one morning, the kitchen still unheated and the saucepan of blue enamel hanging from the wall that I knew my mother's end was near. Her ailment was punctuated by many periods of remission, during which the flame flared up again from the hearth, and the fragrance of fresh bread and melted chocolate wafted under the door at the same time as the paw of the impatient cat. These periods of remission were the occasion for unexpected incidents. My mother and the big walnut cupboard were found at the foot of the stairs where they had both fallen: the former had been trying to transfer the latter in secret from the upper storey to the ground floor. Thereupon my elder brother demanded that my mother take some rest and allow an old servant woman to sleep in the little house with her. But what could an old servant do when faced with a life-force as youthful and malicious as my mother's, so powerful that it could seduce and lead astray a body already half shackled by death? One day, my brother was returning before daybreak, having gone to attend a patient out in the country, when he caught my mother red-handed, committing a most perverse offence. Dressed in her nightgown, but with her big gardening boots on her feet, her little grey septuagenarian's plait done up in a scorpion's tail on the nape of her neck, one foot on the beech-wood trestle, her back arched in the posture of an expert woodman, rejuvenated by an indescribable air of simultaneous delight and guilt, my mother, in defiance of all her promises and the frozen dew, was sawing logs in her backyard.

The 'Marvel'

'It's a marvel! It – is – a – *mar*-vel!'

'I know. She makes sure it is. She does it on purpose!'

My reply earns me an indignant glance from the lady-I-know-a-little. She strokes Pati-Pati's round head one last time before she goes, sighing, 'Begone, my love!' to the tune of 'Poor martyr, understood by none…' My Brussels griffon rewards her with a sentimental sideways glance of farewell – the white of the eye much in evidence, not much brown – and immediately turns her attention to imitating a dog's bark for the amusement of a gentleman stranger who is admiring her. To imitate a dog's bark, Pati-Pati swells out her sunfish cheeks, makes her eyes bulge out of their sockets, sticks out her chest like a shield, and in muted tones proffers a sound that goes something like:

'Goo-goo-goo…'

Then she puffs out her neck, as thick as a wrestler's, smiles, and waits for the applause, before adding a modest:

'Woof.'

If her audience swoons with delight, Pati-Pati, disdaining an encore, satisfies the spectator's demands by modulating a series of sounds in which everyone can recognise the sound of a seal coughing and spluttering, a frog croaking melodiously under the summer shower, and sometimes a klaxon – but never a dog's bark.

At the moment she is mimicking Célimène[50] for a stranger at the dining table.

'Come over here,' says the stranger, wordlessly.

'Who do you take me for?' retorts Pati-Pati. 'Let's have a chat, if that's what you want. That's as far as I'm going.'

'I've got some sugar in my saucer.'

'Did you think I hadn't spotted it? Sugar is one thing, fidelity another. You'll have to be satisfied with my putting a twinkle into this right eye for you, the one that's all golden and ready to drop out, and this left eye, that looks like a marble with a twist of aventurine... Look at my right eye... And my left eye... And now my right eye again...'

I sternly interrupt this mute dialogue.

'Pati-Pati, don't you think that's quite enough, you shameless hussy?'

She comes leaping up to me, with all the devotion of her heart and mind.

'Of course it's enough! As soon as you say so, it's enough! This stranger has nice manners... But you have spoken: and that's enough! What do you expect?'

'We're heading off. Down you come, Pati-Pati.'

She jumps down onto the carpet with a lithe, vigorous leap. When she's standing up, she resembles – wide of girth, with a plump behind and her chest stuck out like a portico – a tiny bay cob. Her black mask laughs, her docked tail transmits its wagging right up to the nape of her neck, and her ears, pricked up heavenwards like horns, ward off any possible ill effects from the evil eye. So she offers herself to the enthusiastic acclaim of the public, my short-haired Brussels griffon, esteemed by breeders as 'a very typical specimen', and by ladies of sensibility as a 'marvel': her official name is Pati-Pati, though she is more generally known among my entourage by the name of 'familiar demon'.

She is two years old, is as merry as a piccaninny, and has the powers of endurance of a champion walker. In the woods, Pati-Pati darts ahead of the bicycle; out in the country, she trots along in the shade of the cart, kilometre after kilometre.

On the return journey, she is still capable of stalking a lizard on the hot flagstones...

'Don't you *ever* get tired, Pati-Pati?'

She laughs like a snuffbox.

'Never! But when I sleep, I sleep for a whole night, and I always lie on the same side. I've never been ill, I've never done my business on a carpet, I've never thrown up, I'm light and airy, free of all sin, as pure as a lily...'

That's true. She's always starving hungry at exactly the time meals are served. She's delirious with enthusiasm when it's time for a walk. She never sits on the wrong chair at table, she is very fond of fish and finds meat much to her taste, she is happy with a crust of bread and swallows her strawberries and mandarins like a connoisseur. If I have to leave her at home, the word 'no' is quite enough; she docilely sits on the landing, hiding her tears. In the metro, she melts away under my cloak, and in trains she makes up her own bed, shaking out a blanket and padding it down in big folds. As soon as the day starts to wane, she keeps a close eye on the garden fence and barks at any suspicious characters.

'Be quiet, Pati-Pati.'

'I'll be quiet,' Pati-Pati replies dutifully. 'But I'm a wild thing when I prowl all the way round our six-metre garden. I poke my head through the bars, I terrorise any shady-looking passers-by, and the cat who's waiting for night to fall so he can scrape up the begonias, and the dog cocking his leg against the ivy-leafed geranium...'

'That's enough of being the watchdog, Pati-Pati: let's go in.'

'Go in?' her whole body cries out. 'Not until I've spent a moment sitting meditatively like the frog in the barrel game just *here*, and then, for just a bit longer, all hunched up and my back arched like a snail's, just *there*... Done it! Let's go in! Have you shut the door? Careful – you've forgotten one of the cats hiding under the curtain: she thinks she's going to be able to spend the night in the dining room... I'll tell her off and turf her out and send her scuttling to her basket. Hop! There she is. Now it's our turn. What's that I hear near the cellar? No, it was nothing. My basket... my bit of flannel over my head... and, more urgently, a hug from you... Thank you. I love you. See you tomorrow.'

Tomorrow, if she wakes up before eight o'clock, she will wait in silence, her paws propped on the edge of the basket, her eyes fixed on the bed. The eleven-o'clock walk finds her ready, and always immaculately turned out. If it's bicycle day, Pati-Pati arches her back so that I can grab her by her skin and lift her into the strawberry basket in front of the handlebars, where she curls up into a ball. In the deserted paths of the Bois,[51] she jumps down: 'Turn right, Pati-Pati, turn right!' In two days she has learnt to distinguish her right – sorry, I mean my right – from her left. She understands a hundred words of our language, knows what time it is without having to look at a watch, knows us by name, waits for the lift instead of taking the stairs up, and after her bath spontaneously offers her belly and back to the electric hairdryer.

If, when I'm working, I spread out my notebooks of tinted paper on my desk, she lies down, silently manicures her nails and dreams away, deferential and motionless. The day a shard of glass wounded her, she herself held out her paw, and turned away her head while it was being bandaged, so that I no longer knew whether I was giving first aid to an animal or to some brave child... When will I ever catch her out? What accident ever placed so much human connivance within the round skull of a tiny dog? They call her 'marvel'. I have to struggle to find anything I could criticise her for...

* * *

Thus grew, in virtue as in beauty, Pati-Pati, the flower of Brabant. In the 16th *arrondissement*, her fame spread so far and wide that for her sake I agreed to a marriage.[52] Her fiancé, when he first approached her, looked like a furious cockchafer:

he had a cockchafer's colour and sturdy back, and his little paws, those of a conqueror, pawed and scratched impetuously at the flagstones. Pati-Pati barely noticed him, and this brief encounter, in which her mind seemed so very far away, was never followed up.

Nonetheless, for the next sixty-five days, Pati-Pati swelled up, assuming the shape first of a sand lizard, with her belly bulging sideways, then that of a rather squashed melon, then…

Two Pati-Patis, tender youths, very small-scale models of the original, now wander around in a basket. Preserved from any traditional mutilation, they wear their tails in hunting-horn style, and their ears like lettuce leaves.

They suckle her abundant milk, but they have to buy it by performing acrobatic tricks that they are really too young to perform. Pati-Pati won't have anything to do with those wallowing hound bitches, all belly and teats, who become blissfully absorbed in their august task. She suckles them sitting down, forcing her puppies to adopt the posture of a mechanic flattened under the old banger that's seized up. She suckles them couched like a sphinx, her nose on her paws – 'Too bad! The youngsters will just have to make do!' – and if the telephone rings, off she trots to where the noise is coming from, towing along the two nursling puppies glued to her breasts. They continue to feed, quite forgotten, full of life; they feed at random, and prosper in spite of their mother and her human, all-too-human concern for all human activities.

'Who phoned? I can hear the car… Where's my collar? Your bag and gloves are on the table, we're going out, aren't we? Someone rang! Are you taking me to *Le Matin*?[53] I can feel it's time… What's that dragging along under me? That little dog again! I keep meeting him everywhere… And then there's that other one, so… He's taken over the whole house. They're nice little things? Hmph!… yes, nice enough. Let's be off, let's be off, come on, get a move on... I'm keeping an eye on you, just in case you were thinking you could go without me...'

Pati-Pati, my friends will always call you 'marvel of marvels' and 'perfection'. I don't protest. But now I know what's wrong with you: you don't like animals.

Bâ-Tou

I'd captured her at the Quai d'Orsay,[54] in a big office of which she was, together with a piece of Chinese embroidery, the most magnificent adornment. When her ephemeral master, who found such a lovely gift rather burdensome, telephoned me, I found her sitting on an ancient table, her backside plumped down on various diplomatic documents, busy with her personal hygiene. Her brows contracted when she saw me, and she jumped to the ground, where she began padding up and down like a wild beast, from the door to the window and from the window to the door, with that way of turning and changing step when encountering an obstacle that is proper to her and all her brothers. But her master chucked a ball of crumpled paper at her and she started to laugh, with an extravagant leap that expended her unused energies and showed her in all her splendour. She was as big as a spaniel, with her long muscular thighs slotted into broad haunches, and her body tapering at the front; she had a rather small head, and ears lined with white fur, painted on the outside with black and grey drawings reminiscent of those that decorate the wings of crepuscular butterflies. A small disdainful jawbone, a moustache as rigid as the dry dune grass, and amber eyes set in black frames – eyes with a gaze as pure as their colour, eyes that never flinch at a human gaze, eyes that have never told a lie... One day, I tried to count the black spots embroidering her coat that was the colour of wheat on her head and back, and ivory-white on her belly: I lost count.

'She comes from Chad,' her master told me. 'She could also come from Asia. She's probably an ounce. Her name is Bâ-Tou, which means "the cat", and she's twenty months old.'

I took her with me; however, she kept gnawing at her travelling crate and sticking her paw out between the slats – a paw that was sometimes open and sometimes closed, like a sensitive marine flower.

I had never possessed such a natural creature at home. Daily life demonstrated that she was still intact, safeguarded from all the assaults of civilisation. A spoilt dog is calculating and mendacious, a cat pretends and conceals. Bâ-Tou hid nothing. She was bursting with health and gave off a nice smell, and her breath was fresh – I could have said that she behaved like a sweet and innocent child, if there was such a thing as sweet and innocent children. The first time she started to play with me, she seized my leg in a strong grip, trying to knock me over. I spoke to her roughly and she let go: she bided her time and then tried again. I sat on the ground and gave her a punch on her lovely velvety nose. She was surprised and stared at me questioningly: I smiled at her and scratched her head. She fell in a heap on her side, uttering a low purr, and offered me her exposed belly. She went mad with joy when I gave her a ball of wool in reward: of how many lambs, taken from the meagre pastures of Africa, could she recognise the odour, now faint and chill?...

She slept in a basket, did her business in the sawdust-filled basin like a well-trained cat, and when I stretched out in the warm water, her laughing and fearsome head appeared, with her two paws, on the edge of the bath...

She loved water. In the morning I would often give her a basin full of water, which she emptied with great swipes of her paws. Drenched and happy, she would start to purr. She would gravely walk up and down with a stolen slipper between her teeth. She would drop her wooden ball down the narrow stairs twenty times, and race down to bring it back up. She would rush up when she heard her name, 'Bâ-Tou', uttering a charming, gentle cry, and lie dreamily ensconced, her eyes wide open and nonchalant, at the feet of the chambermaid as she sat sewing. She ate unhurriedly and delicately picked up the meat with the tips of her paws. Every morning, I presented my head to her: she hugged it with all four paws and rasped its trimmed hair with her rough tongue. One morning, she hugged my bare arm too tight, and I scolded her. She was offended, and jumped on me: I felt on my shoulders the disconcerting weight of a wild beast, her teeth, her claws... I summoned up all my strength and flung Bâ-Tou against a wall. She broke out into a fierce din of caterwaulings, she howled her war cry and jumped at me again. I used her collar to throw her against the wall, and struck her in the middle of her face. At that moment she could admittedly have inflicted a grave injury on me. She didn't, but restrained herself, looked me in the eyes and reflected... I can swear that it wasn't fear that I read in her eyes. She *chose*, at that decisive moment; she opted for peace, friendship, a faithful alliance; she lay down, and licked her warm nose...

When I miss you, Bâ-Tou, I add to my nostalgia the mortifying knowledge that I drove away from my home a friend, a friend who – thank God – was in no way human. It was when I saw you standing on the garden wall – a four-metre high wall, to the top of which you could leap in a single bound – busily bad-mouthing a few terrified cats, that I began to tremble. And then, on another occasion, you came up to the little bitch I was holding on my knees, and measured, on her ear, the exact position of some mysterious fountain which you licked and licked, before probing with your teeth, slowly, your eyes closed... I understood what you were up to, and I merely told you, in a low tone, and a sorrowful voice, 'Oh! Bâ-Tou!...' and you shuddered from head to tail, with repressed shame and avidity.

Alas, Bâ-Tou! The simple life and the tenderness of wild beasts are so difficult for you in our climate... The Roman sky now shelters you; a ditch, too wide for you to leap across, separates you from those people who go to taunt the big cats in the zoo; and I hope that you have forgotten me. For I allowed you – even though I knew you were innocent of everything except your race – to be turned into a caged animal.

Bellaude

'Madame, Bellaude has run away.'

'When did it happen?'

'This morning, as soon as I opened the house. There was a black-and-white waiting for her at the door…'

'Good Lord! Let's hope she'll come back this evening…'

So, she's gone. Apart from the fact that this is the month set aside for canine love affairs, nothing suggested that she was about to take flight; she followed us unfailingly and devotedly, looking lovely in her black and flame-coloured Bas-Rouge[55] coat, her nonchalant amble making her rear paws waggle her double dewclaws like pendants. She sniffed and munched at the grass, and disdainfully avoided the circular frenzy of the Brussels griffons. And then, one day, she came to a halt, joyously pointed her ears, and stared fixedly at a distant point; her whole body exclaimed, in the clear language of a bitch dog:

'Ah, there he is!'

By the time we'd asked her, 'Who?' she was two hundred metres away, since she'd seen him, him, *Him* – some diminutive, yappy, yellow runt…

She – being herself long and light as a doe, tall and proud-necked – seeks dwarves, mongrel fox terriers and basset hounds, false terriers, quivering and minuscule spitzes. Above all others she loves a white poodle that for several winters has been concealed under a muddy coat of snow which no summer can melt. He hangs around my Bas-Rouge with all the resigned fervour of an old scholar. He gazes at her from below, as if peering over his glasses, through his ill-kempt white hair. He escorts her: that's as far as he goes – and he trots along behind her at his ambling little pace that shakes all his skeins of dirty white hair.

So, she's gone. Where? For how long? I have no anxieties about her being run over or stolen; whenever a stranger's hand reaches out towards her, she snakes her neck away and bares her teeth in such a fashion as to disconcert the most resolute. But there are lassos, dog pounds…

A whole day goes by.

'Madame, Bellaude hasn't come home.'

It rained last night, a gentle rain that already harbingers the spring. Where's that hussy got to? She'll have to go without food; but she can drink all right: the streams are flowing with water and the woods are shimmering with puddles.

A small, wet dog stands guard outside my door, by the garden fence. He too is waiting for Bellaude… In the Bois, I ask my friend the guardian whether he hasn't seen the big black bitch with flame-coloured paws, eyebrows and cheeks… He shakes his head.

'I haven't seen anything like that. Come to think, what *have* I seen today? Not much. Nothing at all, to tell you the truth. A lady having a quarrel with her husband, and a gentleman in polished shoes who asked me whether I might know of two rooms to be let in one of the guardians' houses, seeing as how he was homeless… As you can see, nothing out of the ordinary.'

Another day goes by.

'Bellaude's still not back, Madame.'

I set off for my half-past-eleven walk, with the intention of going round the shady woods of Auteuil. A secret springtime quivers in the wind, which is biting when the breeze rises but mild and gentle when it drops. No sign of a black and flame-coloured bitch, but I do see the horns of future hyacinths and the already broad leaf of the cuckoo pint. And here comes the lost, famished bumblebee staggering about on the damp moss: you can warm him up in your hand at no risk of being stung. On the elder trees, at every fork of the branches, a fresh new tuft of tender greenery spurts forth. And six years have taught me to recognise in the raucous trill, the brief descending chromatic scale that a bird's throat pours forth as soon as February arrives, the voice of the great singer, an Auteuil nightingale faithful to his grove, a nightingale whose voice, in the springtime, illumines the nights. Above my head, he is this morning relearning the song that he forgets every year. He starts his imperfect chromatic scale over and over again, interrupting it with a sort of hoarse guffaw; but in a few notes there already ring out the crystal chimes of a night in May, and, if I close my eyes, I can summon up, in spite of myself, through this song, the heavy perfume that drifts down from the flowering acacias...

But where is my dog? I walk past a palisade of chestnut planks, I cross some tripwires placed just above the ground, then I stumble against a chestnut fence, at the end of which there awaits me... a tripwire. What perverse solicitude has set up these palisades and tripwires, both of them dangerous, to discourage lovers of the countryside and break the bones of people out walking? I retrace my steps, tired of having to step past fortifications, and walk along a chestnut palisade that is, I swear it, protecting another palisade which itself serves as a rampart, a little further on, to a wooden fence painted in green... And they accuse the city authorities of neglecting the Bois!

Something stirs behind one of those horrid fences... Something black... flame-coloured... white... yellow... It's her! It's my dog!

Blessings on you, municipality! And you tutelary barricades! And you providential enclosures! It's not just my dog who is sheltered from cars: there are another – one, two, three, four, five – five dogs gathered round her, muddy, some of them bleeding from their battle-wounds, all panting, exhausted; the biggest of them doesn't reach thirty centimetres at the withers...

'Bellaude!'

She hadn't heard me coming, she was playing the part of Célimène.[56] Virtuous in spite of herself, inaccessible only by chance, she loses face at the sound of my shout and all at once bows low, recalled to her condition of servility...

'Oh, Bellaude!...'

She crawls imploringly. But I am not yet ready to forgive her and simply point dramatically across the abolished fortifications to the path of home and duty... She doesn't hesitate, but leaps over the palisade and easily outdistances, in a few strides, the mob of pygmies that follow after her, tongues hanging out...

What have I gone and done? What if Bellaude were going to encounter on her path a seductive figure, tall of stature...

'Madame, Bellaude is back.'

'With five small dogs?'

'No, Madame, with one big one.'

'Good Lord! Where is he?'

'Over there, Madame, on the embankment.'

Yes, there he is, and I remember, with a sigh of relief, that the song says, 'A matching pair is what you need...' The one who's waiting for Bellaude is a Great Dane, with an obtuse stare, passive in his collar and his muzzle of green leather, and as heavy, as broad and as tall – may chance be thanked! – as a calf.

The Two Mother Cats

He's only a young cat, the offspring of the love – the ill-matched union – of Moune, a blue Persian cat, and some anonymous striped tomcat or other. God knows how many striped cats there are in the gardens of Auteuil! On days when an early spring is in the air, at the times when the earth, as it thaws, lies steaming in the sunlight and spreading its fragrance abroad, certain clumps of bushes, certain well-adorned flower-beds that await the seeds that will be planted and the plants that will be pricked out seem strewn with grass snakes: those striped lords, drunk with the incense wafting from the vegetation, twist and turn on their loins, crawl on their bellies, lash out with their tails and scrape their right cheek and then their left cheek delicately along the ground so as to impregnate it with the promising aroma of spring – in the same way that a woman dabs, with her fingertip moistened with perfume, that secret corner just under her ear.

He's only a young cat, the son of one of those striped toms. He bears on his coat the stripes of his race, the old marks of his wild ancestor. But his mother's blood has cast over these stripes a flaky bluish veil of long hairs, as impalpable as a transparent Persian gauze. He's going to be handsome, then, and he's already a delight to see; we try to call him Kamaralzaman[57] – in vain, since the cook and the chambermaid, who are sensible women, translate Kamaralzaman into Moumou.

He's a young cat, and always looks graceful. He shows interest in a ball of paper; the aroma of meat turns him into a roaring, tiny dragon; and the sparrows dart by too quickly for him to follow them with his eye – but he goes into a trance, seated at the window pane, when they peck at the window. He makes a good deal of noise while suckling, since his teeth are growing… He's a young cat, an innocent who has become involved in a real drama.

The tragedy started one day when Black-Cat-from-Next-Door – doesn't this sound like the name of some peasant nobility? – was bewailing, on the dividing wall, the loss of her children, who had been drowned that morning. She was wailing in the same terrible way as all mothers deprived of their offspring: endlessly, on the same note, barely pausing for breath between each cry, exhaling one never-changing lament after another. The tiny little cat Kamaralzaman, down on the ground, gazed at her. His bluish face was lifted up, his eyes, the colour of soapy water, were blinded by the light, and he no longer dared to play because of that great cry… Black-Cat-from-Next-Door saw him and came sweeping down like a madwoman. She sniffed him, realised that he had the smell of a stranger, groaned – 'Khhh…' – with disgust, lashed out at the little cat, sniffed him again, licked his forehead, recoiled with horror, came back, uttered a tender 'Rrr…' to him – in short, demonstrated her frenzy in every possible way. She didn't have enough time to make up her mind. Like a streak of cloud, Moune arrived, as blue as a storm and even swifter… Having been reminded both that she was in mourning and that she owed respect to territorial boundaries, Black-Cat-from-Next-Door vanished, and her cry, from further away, cast a pall over the whole day…

She came back the next day, as cautious and calculating as a beast of the jungle. She uttered no more cries: instead, she deployed a mute boldness and patience. She waited for the moment when, with Moune satiated, Kamaralzaman was staggering away on his soft paws, padding unsteadily round the gravel paths of the garden. She came with a belly heavy with milk, distended teats that burst through her black fleece, muffled mewlings, and mysterious invitations to come and suckle… And while the young cat fed from her, trampling all over her in a regular rhythm, I saw her closing her eyes, her nostrils quivering like a human being holding back tears.

It was at this point that the real mother appeared, her hair erect on her back. She didn't leap forward straight away, but muttered something in a raucous voice. Black-Cat-from-Next-Door, awoken with a start from her maternal illusion, stood up and responded merely with a long low growl, drawing breath, at intervals, through her crimson-flushed jaws. An imperious and heart-rending insult from Moune interrupted her, and she took a step backwards; but she too uttered words of menace. The terrified little cat was lying between them, its hair sticking up, blue-hued, like the tuft of a thistle. I was amazed that, instead of indulging in an immediate bout of fisticuffs, a feline free-for-all with clumps of hair flying through the air, they had decided to stake their claims and talk it over in a way I could almost understand. But all of a sudden, reacting to a shrill insinuation on the part of Black-Cat-from-Next-Door, Moune leapt forward, yowling 'Ah, I'm not going to put up with that!' and flung herself against her rival. Black-Cat sped away, dashed up the lime tree, dangled from it a while and then swung across the wall – and the mother washed her child, who had been sullied by the strange woman.

Several days went by, during which I observed nothing untoward. Moune, filled with anxiety, wasn't getting enough sleep or eating properly. She was burning up with fever, her nose was dry, she slept on a marble console table, and her milk was drying up. Nonetheless, chubby little Kamaralzaman rolled around on the carpets, as broad as he was long. One morning when I was having my breakfast with Moune, and I was tempting her with some sugared milk and crumbs from my croissant, she quivered, flattened her ears, leapt onto the floor and asked me to open the door in such an urgent way that I followed her. She wasn't wrong: the impudent Black-Cat and Kamaralzaman, the one feeding from the other, both happily entangled together, were lying on the first step, in the shadows, at the foot of the stairs onto which Moune flung herself – and where I caught her up in my arms, floppy and lifeless, like a woman in a faint...

Thus it was that Moune, the Persian cat, lost her milk, resigned her rights as a mother and wet nurse, and contracted her restless melancholy, her indifference to squally weather and her hatred for black cats. She has put a curse on all that wears her dusky fleece, with a white patch on the chest, and you can no longer read any sign of her sorrow on her face. However, when Kamaralzaman comes to play too close to her, she draws in her paws under her exhausted teats, feigns sleep and closes her eyes.

Cats

There are five of them around her, all five of them from the same stock and striped just like their ancestor, the wild cat. One wears his black stripes on a pink background like the plumage of a turtle dove, while the other consists of toast-coloured stripes on a very light brown background, like a wallflower. A third appears yellow, next to the fourth, all bands of black velvet, collars and bracelets, on a silver-grey vest of great elegance. But the fifth one, an enormous creature, is resplendent in his tawny fur with a thousand bands. He has mint-green eyes and the broad hairy cheeks of a tiger.

And the she-cat – Good Lord – it's Blackie! A Blackie like a hundred other Blackies, slender, glossy, with a white patch on her chest and eyes of pure gold. We'd called her Blackie because she is black, just as the grey one is called Grey-Cat and the youngest of the blue Persian cats is called Young-Blue. We didn't exactly exhaust our brains with ingenuity.

January, the month of feline love affairs, mantles the Auteuil cats in their loveliest coats and rounds up thirty or so toms for our three female cats. The garden is filled with their interminable palaver, their battles and their odour of green boxwood. Only Blackie shows any sign of interest in them. It's too soon for Young-Blue and Grey-Cat, who gaze down from aloft at the madness of the males. Blackie isn't feeling too well right now: she won't pursue the matter. She takes her time choosing a bevelled branch from the garden, one that had been lopped down last year so that she can use it first as a toothbrush, then as an ear-scratcher, and finally as a side-scraper. She rubs herself against it, giving herself a good scraping down, and showing every sign of satisfaction. There follows a horizontal dance, during which she imitates an eel out of water. She rolls over, drags herself along on her belly, gets her coat dirty, and the five tomcats accompanying her advance and retreat like a single tom. Often, the magnificent leader of the pack can stand it no longer: he darts forward and raises a heavy paw over the temptress… Immediately, the voluptuous choreographer raises herself erect, smacks her impudent assailant and then hunkers down again, paws tucked back under her belly, with the sour, crabby expression of an old bigot. In vain does the mighty striped cat feign submission and homage to Blackie by falling down, with his paws in the air, quailing and submissive. She sends him back to join the anonymous quintet, and without fear or favour administers a smack to any striped cat, if he should contravene etiquette by getting too close.

This cat ballet has been going on since this morning, under my windows. No cry except the harsh and harmonious 'Rrr…' that from time to time rolls out of the tomcats' throats. Blackie, silent and lascivious, provokes and then punishes, and savours her ephemeral omnipotence. Within a week or so, the same male who now trembles before her, who bides his time and goes without food and drink, will grab her firmly by the neck… But until then, he bows before her.

A sixth striped cat has just made his appearance. But none of the tomcats has deigned to size him up as a rival. Plump, velvety and candid, he lost at an early age any interest in the games of love, and the tragic January nights as well as the clear moonlit nights of June have forever ceased to exert any fateful hold over him. This morning, he feels weary of eating, and tired of sleeping. He steps out in his glossy coat under the wan silvery sun, and displays the rather empty-headed but quite harmless vanity that has earned him his name of Handsome-Lad. He smiles at the bright weather and the trusting sparrows. He smiles at Blackie and her quivering escort. With his limp paw he playfully pats an old tulip bulb that he then abandons in favour of a round gravel path. Blackie's tail lashes out and twists like a snake chopped in half: he darts forward, captures it, nibbles it, and receives half a dozen backhanders, short and sharp enough to disfigure him… But Handsome-Lad, who has been demoted from masculinity, is quite ignorant of all the protocols of love, and is content to administer justice on an eye-for-eye basis. Unjustly beaten, he merely pauses for long enough to swell out his lungs and take a step back, before meting out such vengeance on Blackie that she suffocates and chokes with rage before leaping over the wall to hide her humiliation in the neighbouring garden.

And just as I was about to run over to the aid of Handsome-Lad, fearing the fury of the tomcats, I saw that he was retreating, slowly, majestically and unselfconsciously, between the striped cats who stood there motionless, silent and for the first time deferential in the presence of the eunuch who had dared to best the queen.

The Watchman

Sunday – this morning, the children have very odd expressions on their faces. I've already seen that expression, when they were up in the loft organising a performance – with costumes, masks, shrouds and dragging chains – of their play *The Ghost of the Commandery*,[58] an elucubration which has given them a whole week of fever, night fears and furred tongues, the result of being intoxicated with their own phantoms. But that's an old story. Bertrand is eighteen now, and is planning to reform, as befits a young man his age, the organisation of European finance; Renaud, who is over fourteen, has only one thought in his head: how to put together and take apart engines; and Bel-Gazou is this year forever asking me questions of a distressing banality: 'Will I be able to wear stockings in Paris? Will I be able to have a hat in Paris? Will you curl my hair for me on a Sunday?'[59]

All the same, they all seem to me to be acting strangely, and they are forever gathering in corners to talk in low tones.

Monday – the children don't look well this morning.

'What's wrong with you all?' I ask.

'Nothing at all, Auntie Colette!' cry my stepsons.

'Nothing at all, Maman!' cries Bel-Gazou.

They've certainly got their act together! They've concocted this lie with some care. This is turning serious, especially since this evening, as dusk fell, I overheard this fragment of dialogue between the two boys, behind the tennis court.

'He didn't stop from midnight to three o'clock, old chap.'

'Tell me about it, my friend! From midnight to four o'clock you mean! I didn't get a wink of sleep. He kept going, "Pom… pom… pom…", just like that, so slowly… As if he was walking on bare feet, but very, very heavily…'

They noticed me and dashed up to me like two falcons, with their laughter, their white and red tennis balls, and an affected and voluble scattiness… I'm not going to find out anything today.

Wednesday – when I went through Bel-Gazou's bedroom to get to mine last night at eleven o'clock, she was still not asleep. She was lying on her back, her arms extended along her sides, and her dark eyes were darting here and there beneath her fringe. A warm August moon, waxing in the sky, made the shade of the magnolia sway on the parquet floor and a blue light emanated from the white bed.

'Aren't you asleep?'

'No, Maman.'

'What are you thinking about, all alone like that?'

'I'm listening.'

'What to?'

'Nothing, Maman.'

Just then, I heard, distinctly, the sound of a bare foot treading heavily on the upper storey. The upper storey is a loft where nobody sleeps, and where, once night has fallen, nobody has any reason to go: it leads to the attic in the oldest tower. My daughter's hand, as I held it in mine, suddenly clenched into a ball. Two mice passed in the wall, playing together and uttering birdlike cries.

'Are you scared of mice these days?'

'No, Maman.'

Over our heads we again heard footsteps, and I asked in spite of myself: 'So who can be walking about up there?'

Bel-Gazou did not reply, and her silence made me feel uneasy.

'Can't you hear it?'

'Yes, Maman.'

' "Yes, Maman!" – is that all you can say?'

The young girl suddenly burst into tears and sat up in her bed.

'It's not my fault, Maman. *He* walks about like that every night...'

'Who?'

'The footsteps.'

'Whose footsteps?'

'Nobody's.'

'Good Lord, these children are so stupid! You mean you and your brothers still can't get those stories out of your heads? That's the kind of nonsense that you keep brooding over in every corner? Look here: I'm going to go upstairs. Oh yes: *I'll* give you footsteps on the ceiling!'

On the top landing, swarms of flies, congregated around the rafters, roared like a chimney fire as I passed by with my lamp. A gust of wind extinguished it the minute I opened the loft door. But there was no need for a lamp in this attic with its wide windows, through which the moonlight fell in milky swathes. The midnight countryside was gleaming as far as the eye could see, with its silvery undulations and its ashen-mauve dips, bathed – where the meadows sank deepest – by a river of glistening fog that reflected the moonlight... In one tree, a little sparrow-owl imitated the cat, and the cat replied in kind... But there was nothing walking in the loft, under the criss-crossing forest of rafters. I waited for a good long while, breathing in the short-lived cool of night, the odour of threshed wheat that pervades the loft, and then I went downstairs. Bel-Gazou was so tired she had fallen asleep.

Saturday – I have listened out every night since Wednesday. Someone is walking about up there, sometimes at midnight, sometimes around three o'clock. Last night, I went up and down the stairs to the loft four times, to no avail. At lunch,

I force the children to confide in me: in any case, they're tired of having to pretend they know nothing.

'Listen, my darlings, you're going to have to help me understand something. You're certainly going to find this very funny – even Bertrand, who's got nothing new to learn. Just think: I keep hearing, above Bel-Gazou's bedroom, every...'

They all explode at once.

'I know, I know!' shouts Renaud. 'It's the Commander in his suit of armour: he already used to haunt the place in Grandpa's day, Page told me all about it, and...'

'Don't be silly!' says Bertrand with curt detachment. 'The fact is, these phenomena of individual and collective hallucination have been happening here ever since the time that the Virgin, wearing a blue belt and drawn along by four white horses, rose up in front of Guitras and told him...'

'She said nothing!' wails Bel-Gazou. 'She wrote him a letter!'

'And sent it through the post?' mocks Renaud. 'That's so childish!'

'And your Commander *isn't* childish?' asks Bertrand.

'Sorry!' retorts Renaud, blushing furiously. 'The Commander is a family tradition. Your Virgin is a village fairy tale of the kind you come across everywhere...'

'Listen, children, have you quite finished? Can I get a word in edgeways? There's one thing I do know: in the loft there are footsteps that I can't explain. I'm going to keep watch tonight. We'll find out who's on the prowl, be it beast or man. Anyone who wants to can keep watch with me... Good. Agreed on a show of hands!'

Sunday – insomnia. Full moon. Nothing to report, apart from the sound of footsteps heard behind the half-open door to the loft, and then interrupted by Renaud who, harnessed into a Henri II breastplate and wearing a cowboy's red scarf, flung himself romantically forward, shouting, 'Avaunt! Avaunt!...' Everyone turned on him in disgust, accusing him of having 'spoilt everything'.

'It's odd,' remarks Bertrand with crushing, reflective sarcasm, 'to see how fantasy can unbalance the mind of a teenager, even one educated in English schools...'[60]

'By the way, poor fellow-me-lad!' adds my Limousin daughter, 'You don't say "Avaunt! Avaunt!", you say, "I'm a-going to give you a right bloody thrashing!"...'

Tuesday – we kept watch last night, the two boys and me, leaving Bel-Gazou asleep. The moon was at its full and shed a long trail of white light on which rats had left a few ears of nibbled maize. We stood in the darkness behind the half-opened door, and were bored stiff for a full half-hour while we watched the moon's trail shifting, falling diagonally, and licking at the base of the criss-crossing timberwork... Renaud touched me on the arm: someone was walking at the far end of the loft. A rat skedaddled and darted up a wooden beam, followed by its serpent's tail. The footsteps solemnly approached and I hugged the necks of the two boys.

He was approaching, slowly, with a low but distinct tread that echoed on the ancient planks. He entered – after a period that seemed to go on for ever – the path of the moonlight. He was almost white, gigantic in stature: the biggest night-bird I have ever seen, a great horned owl taller than a hunting dog. He walked along in stately fashion, raising his feet immersed in plumage, those hard bird's feet that sounded just like human footsteps. The upper edge of his wings had the same outline as a man's shoulders, and two little tufted horns, which he could lower or raise, trembled like long grasses in the draught from the skylight. He stopped, threw out his chest and flung back his head, and all the plumage on his magnificent face swelled up around the slender beak and two golden lakes in which the moon was reflected. He turned round, showing his back that was streaked with white and very pale yellow. He must have been a great age, solitary and powerful. He resumed his parade-ground march and interrupted it by a sort of war-dance, his head darting right and left, making fierce demi-voltes that were no doubt meant to scare the rat that had escaped. For a brief moment he thought he had scented his prey, and knocked over a skeletal armchair as if he were brushing over a dead twig. He leapt up in fury, fell back down, and scraped his extended tail against the floorboards. He had the gait of a master, and the majesty of a magician...

He no doubt sensed our presence, since he turned to face us, looking outraged. He unhurriedly made his way back to the skylight, half-opened his angelic wings, emitted a sort of low cooing noise, a brief incantation, then leant onto the air and melted away into the night, assuming its colour of snow and silver.

Thursday – the youngest of the boys is at his desk writing a long traveller's tale. Title: *Hunting The Great Horned Owl in Southern Africa*. The oldest has accidentally left the start of a poem on my work table:

> *Beating wings at night, oppressive vision,*
> *From shadow to light, a great grey apparition...*

Everything's back to normal.

A Bygone Spring

The beak of a pair of shears clicks its way down the rosebush paths. Another replies from the orchard. Before long the feet of the rose bushes will be surrounded on all sides by tender shoots, red as dawn at their tips, green and juicy at their base. In the orchard, the stiff rods of the apricot trees, cut down in sacrifice, will continue to burn their small flamelike flowers for another hour before they die away; and the bees will ensure that none goes to waste...

The hillside is smoking with white plum trees, each of them immaterial and dappled like a bulging cloud. At half-past five in the morning, under the horizontal rays of the sun and the dew, the yellow wheat is unquestionably blue in colour, the rusty earth is red and the white plum trees are copper pink. It's just a passing moment, a magical illusion of the light, which fades with the first hour of the day. Everything grows with a divine urgency. The tiniest little piece of living vegetation pushes upwards, straining to its utmost. The peony, blood-red in the first month, shoots up so rapidly that its scapes and its barely unfolded leaves thrust their way up through the earth, bearing aloft the upper crust and holding it hanging there like a roof that has been rent asunder.

The peasants shake their heads. 'April has plenty of surprises in store for us...' They bend wise brows over this folly, this yearly impetuosity of flower and leaf. They are growing old, and find themselves carried along by the headlong career of a terrible pupil who has learnt nothing from their experience. The tilled valley, still criss-crossed by parallel streams, hoists its green furrows above the floodwaters. Now nothing can stop the asparagus, which has already started to rise to the surface like a mole, nor the torchlike flame of the violet iris. Bird, lizard and insect are all caught up in this furious bid for freedom. The greenfinches and goldfinches, the sparrows and chaffinches all behave, when morning comes, like a whole farmyard gorged with grain soaked in brandy. Companies of birds and pairs of grey lizards flaunt themselves in dance, utter extravagant cries, and indulge in mock battles, coming together and separating right before our eyes, and almost under our hands, on one and the same warm stone: and when the children, drunk with excitement, run aimlessly here and there, mayflies rise and circle round their heads like a crown...

In the midst of this great surge, I stay put. Perhaps I already derive more pleasure from comparing this spring with what it once was than I do from greeting its arrival? My torpor is blissful, but too aware of its weight. My ecstasy is sincere, and spontaneous too, but what's the point of it? 'Oh, those yellow daisies!... Oh, the saponin! And the horns of the arum lilies peeping out...' But the daisy, that wild flower, is a poor flower, and how can the moist saponin, in its tentative mauve, compete with the ardour of the peach? But compete it can, thanks to the stream that watered it, between my tenth and fifteenth years. The slender primrose, nothing but stalk with its rudimentary corolla, still clings by a fragile rootlet to the meadow where I used to pick hundreds of primroses, to 'straddle' them along a string and then tie them together in round balls, fresh projectiles that hit you on the cheek like a rough, wet kiss...

I refrain, these days, from picking daisies and pressing them into a greenish ball. I know the risk I would run if I were to try. Poor rural delights, now half-vanished, I can't even bequeath you to another self... 'You see, Bel-Gazou, like that and then like that, straddling the thread, and then you pull...'

'Ah yes!' says Bel-Gazou. 'But it doesn't bounce; I prefer my rubber ball...'

The shears click their beaks in the gardens. Lock me away in a dark room, and that noise will still convey to me the April sun, stinging the skin, as treacherous as a wine without any bouquet. The beelike odour from the pruned apricot tree enters with the noise, as does a certain anguish, the sense of foreboding attached to one of those slight illnesses one suffers before adolescence, maladies that slowly develop, persist for a while, fade away, are cured one morning and come back one evening… I was ten or eleven, but in the company of my nurse, who did the cooking for us at home, I still indulged in the whims of a nursling child. I was a grown-up little girl in the dining room, but I would dash to the kitchen to lick the vinegar off the lettuce leaves in Mélie's plate: she was my faithful dog, my blond and white slave. It was one April morning that I called to her, 'Come along, Mélie, let's pick the clippings from the apricot tree, Milien is going for the espaliers…'

She followed me, and the young chambermaid, Marie-la-Rose – who fully deserved her name – came along too, even though I hadn't invited her. Milien, the day labourer, was finishing his tasks; he was a handsome, sly-looking lad, unhurried and silent…

'Mélie, hold out your apron so I can put the clippings in it…'

On my knees, I picked up the bundles of apricot clippings, covered with blossoms like stars. Mélie playfully cried 'Hoo!' and threw her apron over my head, wrapped me up in it and rolled me gently over. I laughingly curled up like a child and acted silly, filled with happiness. But I couldn't breathe, and I pushed my way out so suddenly that Milien and Marie-la-Rose, who were kissing, didn't have time to separate, and it was too late for Mélie to hide her conniving face…

The clicking of the shears, the abrupt clatter of the chattering birds' beaks… They all speak of something blossoming, of the unexpectedly early sunshine, of getting sunburnt on your forehead, of chill shade, of an unconscious revulsion, of a child's trust betrayed, of suspicion, of dreamy melancholy…

The Seamstress

'Your daughter is nine years old,' one of my friends said to me, 'and she still can't sew? She needs to learn to sew. And when the weather's bad, it's better for a child of her age to busy herself with a piece of sewing than with some storybook.'

'Nine years old? And she doesn't sew?' another friend said to me. 'At eight, my daughter embroidered this place mat for me – look… Oh, it's not particularly fine work, but still, it was nice of her. Now my daughter cuts out her own petticoats… You see, I won't have holes being patched up with pins in my house!'

I docilely poured out this domestic wisdom over Bel-Gazou.

'You're nine years old, and you still can't sew? You need to learn to sew…'

I even added, with scant regard for the truth: 'At the age of eight, I remember that I embroidered a place mat… Oh, it wasn't particularly fine work, of course… And then, when the weather's bad…'

So she learned to sew. And although, with her bare suntanned leg tucked away under her, and her torso leaning there comfortably in her swimming costume, she resembles a ship's apprentice mending a net more than she does an industrious little girl, she shows no tomboyish reluctance for her task. Her hands, turned as brown as tobacco juice by the sun and the sea, hem in a very odd way; they make the simple running stitch look more like the zigzag dotted lines of a road map, but she elegantly finishes off the scallops and is a stern judge of other people's embroidery.

She sews, and is kind enough to keep me company if the rain is streaming down over the sea's blurred horizon. She also sews at the scorching hour when the spindle trees amass a dense round shade beneath them. Occasionally, a quarter of an hour before dinner, black in her white dress – 'Bel-Gazou! Your hands and your dress are nice and clean, don't forget!' – she sits down ceremoniously with a square of fabric in her fingers... Then my friends applaud her:

'Just look at her! What a good girl! Well done! Your Maman must be so pleased!'

Her Maman says nothing – one should keep intense joy to oneself. But should one actually feign it? I'll tell the truth: I don't really like my daughter to sew.

When she reads, she returns in a state of perplexity, with flaming cheeks, from the island with its chestful of precious stones, or from the dark castle where a blond orphan child is held captive. She has soaked in a tried and tested poison, whose effects have long been known. If she is drawing or colouring in pictures, a half-spoken song emerges from her, as uninterrupted as the voice of bees buzzing from the privet hedge. The low hum of a busy fly, the slow waltz of a house painter, the refrain of the spinner at her wheel... But Bel-Gazou is silent when she sews. She stays silent for a long time, and keeps her mouth closed, concealing her broad, brand-new incisors – those little saw-edged blades lodged in the moist heart of a fruit. *She* is silent... So let's write the word that fills me with fear: she is thinking.

Some new problem? Some scourge that I hadn't anticipated? Sitting in a grassy combe, or half-buried in the warm sand and gazing vaguely out to sea, I know perfectly well that she's thinking. She thinks with effervescent speed when she is listening, with a feigned, well-bred discretion, to remarks that are being incautiously thrown out over her head. But it seems that with her needlework she has really started to venture down a road filled with risks and temptations, stitch by stitch, point by point. Silence... Her hand armed with its steel dart comes and goes... Nothing can hold back the bold young explorer. When exactly should I utter the 'Hey!' that will brutally bring her enthusiastic momentum to a halt? Ah, those young seamstresses of bygone days, sitting huddled on their hard little stools and enfolded within their mothers' ample skirts! Maternal authority kept them there for years on end, and they stood up only to change the silk skein, or to run away with a stranger who happened to pass by... Philomène de Watteville and her canvas, on which she embroidered the story of the loss and despair of Albert Savarus...[61]

'What are you thinking of, Bel-Gazou?'

'Nothing, Maman. I'm counting my stitches.'

Silence. The needle's point goes in. A big chain stitch follows after it, coarse and uneven. Silence...

'Maman?'

'Darling?'

'It's not just when you're married that a man can put his arm round a lady's waist?'

'Yes... No... It all depends. If they're really close friends, if they know each other really well – you know? As I said, it all depends. Why are you asking me?'

'No reason, Maman.'

Two stitches, ten misshapen chain stitches.

'Maman! You know Madame X*** – is she married?'

'She was married. She's divorced.'

'Oh yes... and Monsieur F*** – is he married?'

'Yes, of course he is – you know he is!'

'Oh yes... And is it enough if just one of the two is married?'

'Enough for what?'

'Enough for them to depend.'

'You don't say "for them to depend".'

'But you just said that it all depended...'

'Is that really any business of yours? Does it concern you?'

'No, Maman.'

I don't persist. I feel that I'm not good at telling fibs, and I'm not pleased with myself. I should have found something else to say, but I didn't.

Bel-Gazou doesn't persist either, she just carries on sewing. She sews and superimposes on the work that she neglects images and associations of names and persons, all the results of patient observation. A little later, other curiosities will come along, other questions, but above all other silences. If only Bel-Gazou were an innocent child, filled with amazement, always asking questions straight out, her eyes wide open!... But she's too close to the truth, and too natural not to know from birth that the whole of nature hesitates in the face of that most majestic and murky of all instincts, and that it is right to tremble, to keep silent and to lie when we come too close to its secret.

The Hollow Hazelnut

Three shells in petal shape, white as mother-of-pearl and transparent as the rosy snow that falls on the apple trees; two limpets like Tonkinese hats with convergent stripes, black on a yellow background; a sort of shapeless, cartilaginous potato, inanimate but concealing a mysterious life and spurting out, if you press it, a crystalline jet of salty water – a broken knife, a stump of pencil, a ring of blue beads and an exercise book filled with transfers that has got soaked in sea water; a very dirty little pink handkerchief... That's all. Bel-Gazou has finished drawing up an inventory of the contents of her left pocket. She admires the mother-of-pearl petals, then drops them and crushes them under her espadrille. The hydraulic potato, the limpets and the transfers deserve no better fate. Bel-Gazou will keep only the knife, the pencil and the thread of beads that are, together with the handkerchief, in constant use.

The right pocket contains little branches of that pinkish limestone that her parents call, God knows why, lithotamnium, when it's so easy to call it coral.[62] 'But it's not coral, Bel-Gazou.' Not coral? And what do *they* know about it – wretches! Anyway: little branches of lithotamnium, and a hollow hazelnut, its side pierced by a hole where the worm has eaten its way out. Along the three kilometres of coastline, there isn't a single nut tree. The hollow hazelnut found on the beach was brought by a wave – from where? 'From the other side of the world,' states Bel-Gazou. 'And it's very ancient, you know. You can tell because it's a rare type of wood. It's a nut of rosewood like Maman's little desk.'

She glues the nut to her ear and listens. 'It's singing. It says: "hoo... hoo..."'

She listens, her mouth half-open, her raised eyebrows touching her fringe of flat hair. When she's motionless like this, and her mind is emptied, as it were, of everything but the object of her attention, she seems almost ageless. She stares unseeingly at the familiar horizon of her holidays. From the vantage point of a ruined thatched cottage, abandoned by the customs officials, Bel-Gazou can take in, on the right, the Pointe-du-Nez, yellow with lichens, striped with the purple hues of a plinth of mussels left exposed at low tide; in the middle, an inlet of the sea, blue as gleaming new metal, cutting deep into the land like an iron axe-head. On the left, a hedge of dishevelled privet in full flower, whose sickly-sweet almond scent fills the breeze as it is deflowered by the frenzied little feet of the bees. The dry sea-meadow comes right up to the hut and its slope conceals the beach where her friends and family are lounging and roasting in the sun. Before long, the whole family will be asking Bel-Gazou, 'But where were you? But why didn't you come down onto the beach?' Bel-Gazou can't understand this obsession with creeks and coves. Why the beach, always the beach, and nothing but the beach? The hut can hold its own perfectly well against that insipid sand: the damp grove of trees exists too, as does the turbid water of the washhouse, and the field of alfalfa no less than the shade of the fig tree. Grown-ups are so consti-tuted that you could spend your life trying to explain things to them – in vain. The same applies to the hollow hazelnut. 'What are you doing with that old nut?' It's better not to say anything, and to hide the nut, sometimes in a pocket and sometimes in an empty vase or in a knotted handkerchief: for in a single instant, impossible to predict, the nut will be stripped of all its virtues. But for the time being it sings, right into Bel-Gazou's ear, that song which keeps her rooted to the spot...

'I can see it! I can see the song! It's as slender as a hair, it's as slender as a blade of grass!...'

Next year, Bel-Gazou will be more than nine years old. She will no longer be inspired to proclaim those truths that so astound her educators. Every day carries her further and further away from her earliest life, so filled with its quick and vital insights, forever mistrustful and haughtily disdainful of experience, sensible advice, and humdrum wisdom. Next year, she will return to the sand that bathes her in its golden glow, to the salted butter and the foaming cider. She will find her ragged thatch waiting for her, and her city-dweller's feet will here put on their soles of natural horn, gradually thickening as they tread across the flints and the rough ridges of sand. But perhaps she will not find again the subtlety she possesses as a child, and the superiority of her senses that can now taste a scent on her tongue, caress a colour and see – 'as slender as a hair, as slender as a blade of grass' – the melody of an imaginary song...

Notes

1. As the next two paragraphs make clear, the two children who were dead at the time Colette wrote *Claudine's House* were Juliette (whose unhappy life is evoked in 'Motherhood': she would commit suicide at the age of forty-eight) and Achille, who became a doctor.

2. 'She' is Colette's mother, Sidonie.

3. Salvator Rosa (1615–73) was an Italian painter of romantic, often wild landscapes.

4. Sido's first husband, Jules Robineau ('The Savage' also known, apparently, as 'The Ape') brought his bride to 6, rue de l'Hospice, Saint-Sauveur, a village in northern Burgundy: this was to be Colette's birthplace. Robineau died in 1865, leaving Sido free to marry Captain Jules Colette, with whom she may already have been having an affair: the Captain was Colette's father.

5. The term 'lumachella marble' is used to refer to any marble that contains small fossil shells.

6. 'Flick' is the fat round a pig's kidneys.

7. The Captain's reading is typical of a liberal, scientifically minded nineteenth-century bourgeois: *Le Temps* was a newspaper, forerunner of today's *Le Monde*; *Le Mercure de France* was a literary forum; *La Nature* was a science magazine; and the *Revue bleue* seems to have been another literary review.

8. The *Office de Publicité* was a periodical that listed properties (and livestock) for sale.

9. In English in the original.

10. This refers to the French word '*presbytère*'.

11. A rather enigmatic title: the four gospels of the New Testament seem out of place in this secular, rationalist library, while the *Four Gospels* of Emile Zola (*Fecundity*, *Labour*, *Truth*, and the projected but never written *Justice*) were not published until 1901–03.

12. Emile Littré (1801–81) compiled the famous French dictionary; Pierre Larousse (1817–75) also compiled a French dictionary and founded the publishing house that bears his name; Becquerel may refer to one of a dynasty of three scientific writers of the nineteenth century, or may be a misremembered version of Bescherelle – the Bescherelle brothers (Louis-Nicolas and Henri-Honoré) compiled several popular works of reference, including a *Dictionnaire national* (1843).

13. D'Orbigny published a thirteen-volume dictionary of natural history (1843–49).

14. Camille Flammarion (1842–1925) was an astronomer, whose *Astronomie populaire* was published in 1880.

Reclus (1830–1905) took part in the Paris Commune and was banished from France: in exile, he wrote a *Géographie universelle* (94).

16. Eugène Labiche (1815–88) was famous for his farces (especially *The Italian Straw Hat* (1851)); Alphonse Daudet (1840–97), another comic writer, author of *Letters from my Mill* (1869).

17. Prosper Mérimée (1803–70), mainly famous for his short stories such as 'Carmen' (1847).

18. Victor Hugo's *Les Misérables* was published in 1862: Gavroche is one of the characters in it, the type of the streetwise Parisian urchin.

19. Alexandre Dumas *père* (1802–85) is these days best known for his historical novels, of which *Le Collier de la Reine* is one: it is based on a true story of derring-do and intrigue involving Jeanne de la Motte and, among others, Marie Antoinette.

20. Charles Perrault (1628–1703) published his *Mother Goose* tales, based on traditional French fairy tales, in 1697; Gustave Doré (1823–83) was the famous illustrator of this and many other texts (Dante, Milton, Cervantes…).

21. Walter Crane (1845–1915) was an illustrator of children's books. 'The Hind' was originally *La Biche*, a story by Mme d'Aulnoy (1697).

22. François Guizot (1797–1874), prime minister under Louis Philippe, and also a historian.

23. The *Travels of Anacharsis the Younger in Greece* (1788), by the Abbé J.-J. Barthélemy (1716–95), was a guide to ancient Greek culture.

24. The *History of the Consulate and the Empire* was written by Adolphe Thiers (1797–1877): like Guizot he combined a life in politics with a career as a historian. The *quais* here referred to extend along the banks of the Seine where second-hand books are sold.

25. The Duc de Saint-Simon (1675–1755) chronicled the later years of life at the court of Louis XIV.

26. A reference to the *Index librorum prohibitorum*, the list of books banned by the Roman Catholic Church.

27. Emile Zola (1840–1902) was still controversial for his naturalistic depictions of, in particular, working-class life (in e.g. *Germinal*) and sexual transgression (*The Sin of Father Mouret* and *Doctor Pascal*, in which the doctor takes his niece as his mistress). Hugh Shelley identifies the book that Colette stole as *La Joie de vivre* (1884). The 'yellow alluvial deposits' are presumably so-called because of the yellow covers of the first editions (many French books of this period had such covers – cf. the 'yellow book' in Wilde's *The Picture of Dorian Gray*, which Wilde later identified as Huysmans' *A Rebours*).

28. Georges Ohnet (1848–1918) was a best-selling writer.

29. Orris root is the root of the iris, used to make perfumes.

30. Paul Pellisson (1624–93) was imprisoned by Louis XIV in the Bastille: he trained a spider to respond to the sound of a bagpipe by coming down from its web and eating flies off Pellisson's knee.

31. This was Léo.

32. 'Pigeon' was the trade name for this type of lamp.

33. This was one of three gardens belonging to Colette's house.

34. These are all (more or less) classic texts by Alphonse Daudet (*Froment jeune et Risler aîné*), Stendhal (*The Charterhouse of Parma*), Alexandre Dumas *père* (*The Vicomte de Bragelonne*), Octave Feuillet (*Monsieur de Camors*), Oliver Goldsmith (*The Vicar of Wakefield*), Prosper Mérimée (*A Chronicle of the Reign of Charles IX*), Emile Zola (*La Terre*), Alfred de Musset (*Lorenzaccio*), Catulle Mendès (*Les Monstres parisiens* [The Monsters of Paris] and *Grande Maguet*), and Victor Hugo (*Les Misérables*).

35. These literary reviews could be of some sophistication (the *Revue des Deux Mondes* provided a platform for Balzac, Hugo, Sand and others). Ponson du Terrail (1829–71) was a prolific writer of short novels about a character called Rocambole, who gave his name to the French adjective '*rocambolesque*', meaning extravagant, incredible.

36. Catulle Mendès (1842–1909) was a writer in many genres. Hugh Shelley points out that he was one of the first people to realise that it was Colette rather than Willy who had created the character of Claudine.

37. Octave Feuillet (1821–90), novelist, author of e.g. *Monsieur de Camors* (see note 34 above).

38. Captain Colette had been appointed as the guardian of Sidonie's children by her first marriage, Juliette and Achille, but seems to have got his finances in a muddle, despite being a tax collector.

39. *The Tower of Nesle* was an 1832 historical melodrama by Dumas *père* (1802–70).

40. *Denise* was an 1885 play by Dumas *fils* (1824–95).

41. *Hernani*, the play by Hugo (1802–85) that caused a riot when first staged in 1830.

42. *M. Poirier's Son-in-Law* was an 1854 comedy by Emile Augier (1820–89) and Jules Sandeau (1811–83). *Le Bossu* [The Hunchback] was an 1862 play by Paul Féval (1816–87) and Anicet Bourgeois (1806–71). *Les Deux Timides* [Two Timid Fellows] was an 1860 comedy vaudeville by Eugène Labiche and Marc Michel (1812–68).

43. St John's day is 24th June, often counted as Midsummer's Day.

44. Jean-Baptiste Greuze (1725–1805) was a painter who specialised in pictures of winsomely sentimental girls.

45. A chechia is a round, brimless woolly cap.

46. Emile-Alexandre Taskin (1853–97) was a famous baritone.

in-Tin-Tin was an Alsatian dog, the hero of many silent films – he became a popular mascot (in metal and china).

48. The Benoîtons were the much derided upper-class family in the play *La Famille Benoîton* (1865) by Victorien Sardou (1831–1908).

49. Ybañez seems to be a character in a historical novel serialised (as a *feuilleton*) in the newspaper: the story is set in the reign of Louis XIII (note the reference to Cardinal Richelieu).

50. Célimène is the coquette in Molière's *Misanthrope* (1666).

51. The Bois de Boulogne, the big park on the west side of Paris.

52. Colette lived in the chic 16th *arrondissement* with her second husband, Henry de Jouvenel.

53. *Le Matin* was the Paris newspaper for which Colette worked as short-story writer during the First World War.

54. The Quai d'Orsay is where the French Foreign Office was sited (and where part of it still is).

55. The Bas-Rouge ('Red-Stocking') is a breed of dog also known as Beauceron or French Shorthaired Shepherd.

56. See note 50 above.

57. Possibly a reference to a character from the *Arabian Nights*.

58. A commandery was an estate or manor belonging to the society of the Knights Hospitallers.

59. Bertrand and Renaud de Jouvenel were Colette's stepsons, Bel-Gazou was her nickname for her daughter Colette de Jouvenel – a nickname which her own mother (Sido) had given her.

60. As was Bel-Gazou.

61. In Balzac's novel *Albert Savarus* (1842), the heroine was originally called Philomène de Watteville: she is a silent, vengeful character.

62. Lithotamnium is a kind of alga that resembles coral.

Biographical Note

Sidonie-Gabrielle Colette was born in 1873 in Saint-Sauveur-en-Puisaye, a village in the Burgundy region of France. Her childhood in the countryside appears to have been an idyllic one, largely thanks to the kind and protective attentions of her mother Sido. In 1893 she married Henri Gauthier-Villars, known as 'Willy', a notorious Parisian socialite who began publishing ghost-written articles and books under his own name and forced his wife to write a book of childhood memoirs for him, which appeared in 1900 as *Claudine at School*. The book was a resounding success for Willy, and he made her write three more Claudine novels in quick succession – *Claudine in Paris* (1901), *Claudine Married* (1902) and *Claudine Takes Off* (1903) – followed by *Minne* (1904) and *Egarements de Minne* (1905). She left Willy in 1906 – they divorced four years later – and controversially started earning her living as a transvestite dancer in the Moulin Rouge and various other Parisian and provincial venues. She began writing for the newspaper *Le Matin*, of which she became the literary director in 1919. In 1912 she married Henri de Jouvenel, the newspaper's publishing director, with whom she had a daughter named Colette the following year. During the First World War she worked as a night nurse for the wounded in a Parisian school. She continued to write and publish novels and stories on a regular basis, such as *The Vagabond* (1911), *Claudine's House* (1922) and *Green Wheat* (1923 – the first book she published under her own name). She was also involved in theatre, writing successful plays, notably *Chéri* and *The Last of Chéri*, and often acting in them herself. Her literary achievements saw her awarded many prestigious prizes and honours – including the Légion d'Honneur and a chair in the Royal Academy of Belgium – but her controversial lifestyle and choice of subject matter often caused scandal among the more conservative sections of society. She married her third husband Maurice Goudeket in 1935, who, since he was Jewish, was arrested and detained by the Nazis in 1941. Colette managed to obtain his liberation in 1942. After the War, she was voted into the prestigious Académie Goncourt, becoming its president in 1949. Her health deteriorated in the late 1940s and she died in 1953, receiving a full state funeral, even though the Catholic Church refused to bury her, on account of her two divorces and her showgirl past.

Andrew Brown studied at the University of Cambridge, where he taught French for many years. He now works as a freelance teacher and translator. He is the author of *Roland Barthes: the Figures of Writing* (OUP, 1993), and his translations include *Memoirs of a Madman* by Gustave Flaubert, *For a Night of Love* by Emile Zola, *The Jinx* by Théophile Gautier, *Mademoiselle de Scudéri* by E.T.A. Hoffmann, *Theseus* by André Gide, *Incest* by Marquis de Sade, *The Ghost-seer* by Friedrich von Schiller, *Colonel Chabert* by Honoré de Balzac, *Memoirs of an Egotist* by Stendhal, *Butterball* by Guy de Maupassant and *With the Flow* by Joris-Karl Huysmans, all published by Hesperus Press.